Even If It Kills Me

Even If It Kills Me

Dorothy Joan Harris

Cover by Carol Wakefield

Scholastic Canada Ltd.

Scholastic Canada Ltd.
123 Newkirk Road, Richmond Hill, Ontario, Canada L4C 3G5

Scholastic Inc.
555 Broadway, New York, NY 10012, USA

Ashton Scholastic Limited
Private Bag 92801, Penrose, Auckland, New Zealand

Ashton Scholastic Pty Limited
PO Box 579, Gosford, NSW 2250, Australia

Scholastic Publications Ltd.
Villiers House, Clarendon Avenue, Leamington Spa,
Warwickshire, CV32 5PR, UK

Canadian Cataloguing in Publication Data

Harris, Dorothy Joan, 1931
   Even if it kills me

ISBN 0-590-73829-1

1. Anorexia nervosa - Juvenile fiction.
I. Title.

PS8565.A6483E87 1991   jC813'.54   C91-005233-6
PZ7.H37Ev 1991

8 7 6 5 4   Printed in Canada   4 5 6 7/9

For Andrea,
who has been there

Contents

1
The birthday locker

Sometimes I wonder just when it all began. Did it start with what Dad said to me? Mom thinks so; she thinks it's all his fault. And Dad says no, if anybody started it, she did. After all, she's the one who's always dieting and fussing about how she looks. And about how Katie and I look too. So it's mostly her fault, he says.

But I know they're both wrong. It's not anybody's fault, really. Not even mine.

*　　*　　*

There wasn't anything special or different about that spring. Dad was away a lot, as usual. He's vice-president of an importing company, so he has to make business trips all over North America and often to Europe too. He says he doesn't enjoy traveling, that it isn't as glamorous as it sounds and he'd rather stay home. I'm not sure whether I believe him. Mom certainly doesn't. She complains to us about how much he's away from home. But whenever she complains to Dad he says, "Well, just remember — it's my job that pays for this house and the new living room furniture, to say nothing of all the clothes you buy for yourself and the girls." And then there's not much Mom can say. Because she does like those things. She likes having nice clothes, and well-dressed children, and an elegant house. There's never anything shabby or out of place in *our* house.

Except in Katie's room, of course. Katie is my older sister. Not much older, we're only fifteen months apart. But we couldn't be more different from each other if we were fifteen years apart. We look different: I have dark eyes and dark hair with bangs, her hair is light with a curly perm in it. And we act even more different. For one thing, Katie is allergic to any foods with additives and if she eats the wrong kind of food she gets hyperactive. That means she can't sit still, she yells instead of talking and loses her temper over the slightest thing. Mom spends a lot of time battling with Katie, and she tries to keep any foods with additives out of the house. But that doesn't help when Katie eats junk food at a friend's house. And even when Katie hasn't eaten anything bad for her, she still blows up easily.

I'm just the opposite. I hardly ever yell. It's

not that I don't get angry — I do, lots of times. But even when I'm really mad at someone I usually don't let on. Partly because I don't want to be like Katie. And partly because of all the times Mom has told me that nice girls don't yell. I guess Katie doesn't care about that. Mostly, though, it's because I like to hear Mom say, "Oh Melanie, I'm glad you're such a good child. I couldn't take another daughter like Katie."

Mom says that to me a lot. She said it again one morning just after Dad had left on one of his trips. We'd gotten up early to say good-bye to him, and then Katie had stormed around the kitchen all through breakfast, trying to talk Mom into buying her a new sweater.

"But Mom," Katie argued, "I just know Anthony is going to ask me to his party on Saturday. I can just feel it! And you know how gorgeous Anthony is!"

"Well, if he does ask you, you can go," Mom said in a soothing voice. "But you have plenty of clothes to choose from already."

"I don't have anything nearly as nice as that silver boucle sweater you just bought."

"Katie, my boucle sweater is far too grown-up for you," Mom answered firmly. She tried to switch the subject. "You haven't had much breakfast yet — sit down and finish your cereal."

I was keeping out of the whole discussion, so I'd finished my cereal and was making some toast. I knew Mom would never let Katie borrow her new sweater. Katie usually managed to spill food or pop on any clothes she borrowed. Thank goodness my tops were too small for her, I thought to myself.

"Anyway," Mom was going on, "you have your new pink blouse, the one with the frilly collar. You can wear that to the party."

Katie stopped flouncing about and plunked herself down in a chair. "No, I can't."

"Why not?"

"Well," she muttered, "it fell on the floor in my closet and got all wrinkled, so I figured I'd just give it a quick press and — "

"Oh, Katie!" Mom gave an exasperated sigh. "And I suppose you had the iron too hot again."

"Well, I was in a hurry."

"Katie, you know you have to use a cool iron on anything made of polyester! I've told you so often enough. Is the blouse ruined?"

"Just the frill. It sort of melted."

Mom put down her coffee cup and got to her feet. "You'd better show me," she said with another sigh. "If the frill is all that's damaged maybe I can do something. Let's have a look — that blouse was too expensive to throw out."

4

Katie got up and followed Mom upstairs. That left the kitchen a lot quieter. I spread honey on my toast, nice and evenly, and cut it into fingers. Mom used to cut our toast into fingers for Katie and me when we were small, and I still like it that way. Katie's place mat was a mess, I noticed, where she'd spilled her cereal. Now all the place mats would have to be washed.

I could hear Mom and Katie talking upstairs, going through Katie's wardrobe of sweaters and blouses. But suddenly I stiffened. Katie's voice came floating down, saying, "What about that white shaker-stitch sweater of Melanie's? It's so loose it'd probably fit me."

I dropped my toast and flew up the stairs. I got there just as Katie was opening my closet door.

"No, you don't!" I cried. "You leave my clothes alone!"

"I haven't touched your stupid clothes," Katie snapped.

"You were going to! Get out of my closet and get out of my room! You know I don't like you in here."

For once I was yelling myself. Mom quickly stepped in between us.

"Girls, girls!" she said. "Don't shriek like that. People can hear you right out in the street."

I shut up then, but Katie didn't. "Miss Goody-Goody!" she taunted, "With your dumb tidy room. See — I'm putting my hands in my pockets so I won't contaminate a thing."

"Katie, that's enough," said Mom, glancing at her watch. "You're going to miss your bus if you don't hurry. Come and get ready for school now, and I'll see what can be done with that pink blouse."

Mom hurried Katie back downstairs. I could hear her fussing because Katie hadn't finished her cereal, and then the back door slammed. Since my school is only a few blocks from our house, I don't take the bus. Good thing too, because I was too mad to go anywhere with Katie right then. I was mad at Mom too. She should've told Katie to stay out of my closet, I thought. She should've just told her, flat out. She knows I don't like having my room messed up.

I took a quick look around to make sure everything was the way I'd left it and then I went back downstairs. Mom was sitting in the living room with Katie's blouse in her lap.

I still felt mad — but Mom was too busy to notice. I watched her turning the blouse over in her hands, and asked, "Can you fix it?"

Mom pursed her lips doubtfully. "I don't know. I may have to take the collar right off.

That Katie — I've told her to be careful with the iron, but she never stops to think." She glanced up briefly. "I'm glad you're different, Melanie. Are you leaving now?"

"Yes, I want to get to school early today."

"Okay. Have a good day."

Mom gave me a quick peck on the cheek and then turned back to her sewing. I let myself out quietly. If I was the kind of person who slammed doors I'd sure have done it right then. I was sick of Katie, Katie, Katie. If Mom couldn't fix that blouse she'd probably buy Katie something new just to keep her quiet. And she should've made it clear that my clothes were mine. I'd better not grow much more, I thought, or I'd have to put a padlock on my closet.

I was growing a bit . . . uh, bigger. Bigger up top, that is. In fact Mom's bought me what she calls a "starter" bra — but I don't wear it much. A lot of girls at school can't wait to start wearing bras. I see them all the time flaunting them when we change for gym. Flaunting their . . . chests, too. But I don't like wearing my bra and I'm glad Mom doesn't insist on it.

I always walk to school by myself, since no one from my class lives near us. At school I mostly hang around with Rhona Pilcher. We aren't exactly "best friends" — at least, not the kind that you read about in books, the kind that do everything together and talk on the phone for hours and tell each other secrets. I don't have any friends like that. The closest thing to a best friend I have is Dan McLaughlin, who lives next door to us. Dan and I used to play together when we were little kids. And we still spend time together, mostly at his house, where he has a great model train layout in the basement. He's crazy about his model trains — and to tell the truth, I like them too. But Dan is a year younger and behind me in school so I don't see much of him there. And we don't walk to school together, not any more. I guess that's my fault. He still looks like a little kid, you see, and I don't want to be teased about having a little kid as a boyfriend. I don't want to be teased about having any kind of boyfriend at all. So I walk to school alone and then go to classes with Rhona.

Sometimes I think that I don't actually like Rhona very much. There are other girls in my class I think I'd like better. But they all seem to have friends already. And since Rhona and I have lockers side by side and she doesn't have any other friends either, we just keep on walking to classes together.

That day, when I got to my row of lockers, there was a mob of kids at one end. They were all crowding around Valerie Novak and looking at her locker — it had been decorated with red and white streamers and flowers made out of tissues and a big sign that said *Happy Birthday!* That's a tradition at our school — if you have lots of friends, they decorate your locker for you on your birthday as a surprise. Not that I figured this was much of a surprise to Valerie. She knew her friends would make a fuss on her birthday. After all, she's the most popular girl in our class. She's a tall willowy girl, with long straight blonde hair that makes her look more willowy than ever, and she knows how to bat her eyelashes and get boys to fall all over her. Now she was putting on a good act of being surprised.

"Oh, gosh!" she said, looking around at the crowd and smiling coyly. "Isn't that pretty! Who did all this anyway? I'll bet you had a hand in it, Paul!"

She knew darned well that Paul Dunstable would have had a hand in it. He walks her to school every day.

"Yeah, I helped," he admitted. "But Andrea and Tammy made the flowers."

"Oh, did you?" Valerie gushed to the two girls in the crowd. "Did you really?"

The locker beside me slammed and I turned to see Rhona. "Yecch!" she said, with a sneer in

Valerie's direction. "Is she ever laying it on thick. What a phony!"

"Yeah, she sure is," I agreed.

"That whole business is dumb anyway," Rhona went on. "What's so great about having some streamers stuck on your locker door? Who cares — "

At that point the first bell rang. I ducked into my own locker for my books and used that as an excuse not to answer. Because I wasn't going to tell Rhona what I was really thinking. I wasn't going to tell her how much I'd like to be standing in the middle of a crowd of friends just the way Valerie was, how much I'd like to find my locker decorated on my birthday. I wanted that so much that I'd almost have traded my good report cards for it. What's more, I had a birthday coming up before long, at the beginning of May. I could just imagine what it would feel like to come to school and walk down the hallway with my friends — and then spot my locker all decorated. I wouldn't overact, like Valerie was doing. I'd just stand by it and look pleased.

But I don't have a crowd of friends. So even if I asked Rhona to do it for me — which I wouldn't — I'd look pretty silly standing there on my own, staring at my locker, wouldn't I?

I didn't answer my own question either.

When I found my books I hurried off down the hallway without even waiting for Rhona. And without giving another glance at Valerie's brightly colored streamers and flowers and *Happy Birthday* sign.

*   *   *

When I got home from school that day I saw the pink blouse hanging on the back of a chair. Mom had taken the melted frill off and left a plain round collar, which looked fine to me. But whether or not Katie would like it was another matter. If she didn't, she might still have designs on my big white sweater. I'd better hide it for a while, I decided, and went up to my room to put the sweater at the bottom of my underwear drawer, with my pyjamas and nighties folded neatly on top.

I like my drawers kept tidy. I like my whole room tidy. But right then my desk wasn't — it was covered with a science project on "Future Means of Transportation." Science is not my best subject. But our science teacher, Mr. Boucher, likes any project with lots of neat diagrams, so I figured I could still get a good mark that way.

I sat down at my desk with the drawing I was working on and frowned at it for a while. As diagrams go it was neat enough — but it sure didn't look much like an amphibious vehicle of the future. I was still frowning when the phone rang downstairs.

"I'll get it!" I heard Katie shout, on her way in the back door. "Probably Anthony for me!"

I heard her pick up the phone with a bright hello, and then her voice changed. "Melanie! It's Dan," she hollered. "It's your boyfriend."

She sort of sang the last word in a mocking way. I hate when she does that. I hurried down the stairs and grabbed the phone from her. "He's not my boyfriend!" I hissed at her, clamping my hand over the mouthpiece.

"Why not? He's a boy, isn't he?" Katie said innocently. "And a friend?"

"He's a boy . . . friend," I answered, with an angry pause between the words.

"Whatever."

She gave a careless shrug and left. I waited till she was well out of earshot. "Hi, Dan," I said at last.

"Hi, Melanie." If he'd heard our bickering, he wasn't letting on. "Can you come over? I've got a new signal for the train set."

"I'm working on my science project," I told him.

"You've been working on that for weeks."

"I know. But it's going to count for half our

final mark. And I can't get my drawing of an amphibious vehicle to look like anything at all."

"Why don't you bring your drawing over?" he suggested. "Maybe I can help you. And then we can try out the new signal afterwards."

That sounded like a sensible idea, since Dan was pretty smart in science. So I took my diagram over. He studied it for a moment and then said, "That's not bad. Not bad at all."

"It's not good," I replied.

"Well — Boucher will know what you're trying to show. It doesn't have to be perfect."

"But I want it perfect! I want the whole project to be perfect."

"Melanie," Dan's voice took on a patient tone, "you're not going to get a hundred percent on a science project, you know. Nobody ever does."

"I know. It's just that it bothers me if things aren't right."

Dan chewed his lip thoughtfully. "Well," he said, "tell you what. If you want, I'll ask my dad about it tonight. He's an engineer, I'm sure he's got some books or magazines you could look at."

"Oh, would you? Thanks, Dan."

"Sure. No sweat." He turned and led the way down to the basement. "Come on. I've already got hot chocolate made."

Most of the space in the McLaughlins' recreation room is taken up by their train layout. It started out as his father's, but Dan's been allowed to run it for a long time now. There's a huge table, with an intricate pattern of train tracks, and around the tracks there's a whole miniature landscape with roads and trees and tiny houses and train stations. The new signal was for a level crossing: as soon as the train reached a certain point on the track a tiny barrier went down across the road and a sign began to blink, just like at a real crossing. It was neat. Dan let me handle the controls and we made it happen again and again.

I like playing with Dan's trains. Everything is so tiny and — well, perfect. The little black steam engine that pulls the cars is exactly like a real engine, with tiny piston rods that move as the wheels turn. Dan's grandfather sent it to him, all the way from England. I like sitting at the switch and controlling where the trains will go and watching the little steam engine chug along. And I never have to worry about finding something to talk about with Dan. We just sit there and work the trains and we don't even have to talk at all.

And his hot chocolate is good too. Dan puts about six spoonfuls of chocolate powder in each mug when he makes it, and then adds marshmallows as well. It's like a chocolate bar in a mug. So when I finally went home for supper I wasn't very hungry.

That didn't matter though. Supper was sort of skimpy that night. It often is when Dad's just left on a trip.

"Plain old leftover chicken tonight?" said Katie, wrinkling her nose at her plate. "And no cheese sauce for the broccoli?"

"You can put butter on your vegetables," answered Mom.

"You always make cheese sauce when Dad's home."

"That's why I try to serve plainer meals when we're alone. Do you have any idea how many calories there are in cheese sauce?"

"No. I just know it makes broccoli taste better."

"Of course it does, with all the cream and butter and cheese I put in it. That's also why it's so fattening."

"So?" muttered Katie, poking at her food, "I'd rather be fat."

"No, you wouldn't," Mom told her. "Not with the pool opening at the club in a few weeks. You wouldn't like yourself in a bathing suit if you were fat. I'd like to lose a bit of weight myself before I put on a bathing suit again. I figure if I skip breakfast and have plain dinners like this for a while, that should do it. There aren't many calories in chicken and these vegetables are low too — only about 50 calories in each serving."

I tuned out the conversation. Whenever Mom got onto the subject of calories and diets I knew we were in for a really boring time. I nibbled at my chicken and pushed my vegetables around the plate. As soon as I could I excused myself and went up to my room.

I love my bedroom. I'm so glad there's only Katie and me in our family so I can have a place all to myself. And I love the way my room looks: pink wallpaper and curtains and rug; white painted furniture trimmed with gold. I chose the flowered wallpaper myself, and there are flower decals on my dresser and mirror and toy chest. I still have my toy chest and all my stuffed animals too — I keep them piled on top of the chest, except for my white stuffed cat that sits in the middle of my bed. When I'm in my own room, with all my own favorite things, all arranged just the way I like them, I feel . . . safe. Safe and secure, as if nothing bad could ever happen to me. Nothing bad like getting a poor report card, or being the very last one chosen for a team in gym class, or — or getting my period at school when I'm not expecting it. I worry about that a lot. That wouldn't just be bad, it would be awful. And it could happen. My periods are so irregular I never know when the next one might arrive. If that ever happened I'd just die.

I sat down at my desk and spread out my project again. But there was no point going on with my amphibious vehicle until Dan had spoken to his father, so I fiddled with the shading on one of the other diagrams for a bit and then reached over and wound up the little china carousel that sits in the corner of my desk. The carousel had been on my birthday cake the year I was nine. I had wonderful birthday parties when I was in grade school. Mom always let me invite every girl in the class, no matter how many there were, and she always bought a big fancy cake. She'd already been talking about the birthday I had coming up.

"You'll be fourteen this birthday, Melanie," she'd said. "Wouldn't you like a mixed party this year? You could have it in the family room and there'd be room for dancing if you wanted."

I'd put her off with an "I'll think about it." But I already knew I didn't want a party. In the first place I don't know any of the kids in my class well enough to invite them, not even the girls. And certainly not the boys. And even if I did invite a bunch of kids and even if they did come — I wouldn't know how to talk to them. Especially the boys. I can never think of anything to say to a boy.

I sighed, and went back to shading in the diagram. Life was a lot simpler when I was nine, I thought sadly. No projects and no exams. Boys were just creatures that you ran away from on the playground, nobody expected you to talk to them. And as long as you knew how to skip, you could join in the fun with everyone else at recess.

I couldn't help wishing I was nine again.

2
Hospital emergency!

By Saturday morning Katie still hadn't been invited to Anthony's party and she was in a terrible mood. I was glad that it was one of my candystriper weekends. That meant that I'd be out of the house most of the day, working at the hospital.

Candystripers are student volunteers. We're called that because our uniforms are made of red and white striped material. We do a lot of different jobs around the hospital: delivering mail and flowers to the rooms, pushing wheelchairs for patients going for X-rays or special tests, helping the nurses maneuver the stretcher beds and all sorts of other really useful jobs.

Our hospital — it's called Lakeshore General — isn't a bit like the big downtown hospitals. I visited my aunt once in one of the downtown hospitals and it was so huge and confusing and full of hurrying people that I couldn't wait to leave.

19

Lakeshore General isn't like that at all. Sometimes the Emergency Department gets rather crowded, but the rest of the hospital is bright and clean and orderly. I love working there. It makes me feel part of something important. I love seeing the doctors in their lab coats and the nurses in their uniforms all busily working. And I love walking down the halls in my own candystripers' uniform — especially since I've earned my candystripers' cap and badge as well. You have to work a hundred hours to earn each of those, so they really mean something. After all, the work we do saves a lot of nurses' hours, so it *is* important — our supervisor often says so.

Saturday was a gloomy, rainy day. Which made the bright busy hospital seem more pleasant than ever. I was humming to myself as I went to the candystripers' room to hang up my coat and put on my cap, and I stood in front of the mirror longer than I really needed to, just admiring myself. Our uniform is really cute — a striped pinafore with a blouse or sweater underneath. Actually it's always a blouse that we wear underneath; the hospital is too warm for a sweater. But then I guess it has to be warm for the patients in those skimpy blue nightgowns.

That day we had a new girl, Tory, starting as a candystriper.

"Melanie, I'm glad you're on today," our supervisor, Mrs. Sullivan, said to me. "You can show Tory around." She turned and spoke to the new girl. "Melanie is one of our best workers. She never skips a day, and she always looks neat and clean."

Mrs. Sullivan is not one of my favorite people — she's too big and loud and bossy. But even so, it gave me a warm glow to be praised like that. I looked pleased and said, "Hi, Tory."

"Hi," she answered.

I could see why Mrs. Sullivan was stressing that I was neat. Tory's hair was long and straggly and her nails were none too clean.

"Bitsy has phoned in sick," Mrs. Sullivan was going on, "so we're going to be short-handed. Just Sue and Veronica and you two. Melanie, you'd better take Tory with you and get started on the flower deliveries."

"Okay," I answered. "Come on, Tory."

I didn't mind that we were short-handed. I like being busy. But I was disappointed that Bitsy wouldn't be in. She's another new candystriper. When I showed her around she followed my every move with big admiring eyes. Since then she's even changed her hairstyle to a long bob with bangs, like mine. It's nice to have someone admire you like that.

I figured Tory wouldn't be as easy to impress. I led her off to the flower room as I'd been told. There was only one delivery as yet: an arrangement of yellow roses addressed to a Mrs. Amodeo. I looked her up in the patient file, found she was in room 104 on West Surgical, and told Tory to come along. We'd deliver the flowers, I said, and in the process I'd show her around the main floor.

I suppose even our small hospital can be confusing the first time you walk through it, with all its long corridors and various wings. It's not confusing to me anymore. I think by now I could find my way to every single ward and department. I kept pointing places out to Tory as we walked.

Tory didn't say much. She just nodded whenever I said "That's the X-ray department" or "That's the way to Emerg." The only question she asked was about the loudspeaker: the calm voice that you can hear anywhere in the hospital, paging various doctors.

"Does that thing go on all the time?" she asked.

"What thing?"

"That loudspeaker."

"Oh, yes. But after a while you hardly notice it."

Tory raised her eyebrows at me as if she didn't believe that last remark. But she didn't say anything more. We went down another long hallway, to West Surgical. I knocked lightly on the door of room 104 and we went in.

"Flowers for you, Mrs. Amodeo," I said brightly.

It was a private room. A woman was sitting in the chair, in a pale blue velour bathrobe.

"Oh, thank you, my dear," she answered. "How lovely."

I set the roses down on the dresser beside another big bouquet. "And here's the card," I went on, handing it to her. Then I checked the water container of both arrangements with my finger. "There's lots of water in the roses, but your other flowers need some. Shall I do that for you?"

"Yes, please. That's kind of you — thanks so much."

She thanked me some more as we left and I felt a warm glow again. But on our way back to the candystripers' room Tory began to complain.

"You sure have to walk a lot in this job, don't

you?" she said. "We must've walked nearly a mile already."

"Well, sure," I told her. "But you get used to it." I glanced down at her flimsy ballerina-type slippers. "You'd be better off in comfortable shoes. White running shoes are best, as long as they're clean."

"And is this all we do?" Tory went on. "Just act as delivery girls?"

"No, not all. We do anything that saves the nurses time."

I thought to myself that Tory probably wouldn't last long as a candystriper. A lot of girls don't. Sometimes it's because they expect to do glamorous exciting things all day. Other girls are put off by the sight of really sick people or badly hurt ones. And sometimes girls are simply let go — if you miss two Saturdays in a row without a good reason, for example, you're out. So far, even though we work two Saturdays every month, I hadn't missed a single day.

By now more flowers had come in, as well as some cards, and we delivered them — with more walking. And then I figured it was time for our morning break.

I always like going to the hospital cafeteria. It doesn't even cost us anything, because candystripers are given tickets each morning good for one drink at our morning break and one complete lunch. So I led Tory off to the cafeteria — I noticed she didn't complain about the walk this time — and we got in line.

There were two doctors in their green operating room outfits ahead of us. I could hear them discussing the operation they'd just done. I love to eavesdrop on conversations like that, but you don't get much chance to because the doctors and nurses sit in a separate alcove off the main cafeteria. I didn't see any other candystripers at the tables, just some groups of ward aides in their blue coveralls and some women volunteers in their pink smocks, so Tory and I took a place over by the window.

After we sat down I spotted our own family doctor, Dr. Vosch, in the line. He looked very sharp, as always, in carefully pressed pants and a crisp white lab coat. I was sorry we weren't still in line. He's always friendly when he sees me at the hospital, and I thought that might impress Tory. But he didn't notice me at all.

Mrs. Sullivan did though, as soon as we got back to the candystripers' room. She pounced on us.

"Where have you been?" she demanded loudly.

"Just — just on our break," I stammered.

"Well, you've been gone a long time — they're waiting for a wheelchair in West Medical. You get a wheelchair from Transport, Melanie, and hurry along to room 122. And Tory, you stay here to answer the phone. I have to pick up a package at the front desk."

Mrs. Sullivan stormed off down the hallway. Without another word I went off in the other direction, my cheeks flaming. *We didn't spend too long in the cafeteria!* I told myself angrily. *And we're allowed a break; she had no right to blow up at me like that!* Even though I don't like Mrs. Sullivan that much, it upset me to have her get mad at me. My cheeks were still hot after I'd collected the wheelchair and arrived at room 122.

Through the open door I could hear an argument going on.

"I don't need any tomfool wheelchair!" a red-faced man in the bed was yelling.

"It's hospital regulations, Mr. Tanner," the nurse in the room replied. "All patients have to be in a wheelchair to go anywhere off the ward." Her voice was sharp, as if she'd said that a few times already.

"Then the regulations are stupid!" the man snapped. "I can walk perfectly well by myself."

Men patients are often like that. They don't like the idea of being pushed in a wheelchair. It doesn't look masculine, I guess. I've even had one man who wanted me to sit in the wheelchair while he pushed. Finally, though, the nurse persuaded Mr. Tanner to get into the wheelchair. His face was redder than ever by then, and he was still grumbling in a loud voice as I started off with him to the X-ray department.

After I turned the corner the grumbling stopped. I was glad of that, since it was rather embarrassing. But then I got a queer feeling. He was too quiet now. I stopped, and stepped around the wheelchair to look at his face. It wasn't red any more; it was turning a strange shade of gray.

"Mr. Tanner?" I called. "Mr. Tanner? Are you all right?"

He didn't answer. I looked around in a panic. We were in the long corridor that borders the garden quadrangle, and there wasn't a nurses' station in sight. There wasn't anyone around at all, except a rather slight young woman walking a few yards ahead of us. With her dark hair caught back in a big barrette, she didn't look very old — but she was wearing a white lab coat so she could be a doctor, I thought. I ran to catch up with her.

"Excuse me," — my voice came out as a squeak — "are you a doctor? This man I'm taking down to X-ray . . . he's turning a strange color."

The young woman looked back to where I was pointing. Then her eyes widened and she moved.

"Quick!" she said to me, "The back door of Emerg — up there! Open it for me."

She ran back and grabbed the wheelchair while I hurried ahead. Luckily I knew what door she meant even though it wasn't marked. I yanked it open and held it. Then, as she was wheeling Mr. Tanner through it, she said, "Now run ahead to the nurses' station and warn them it's a cardiac arrest."

I sped through the hallway to the desk where a nurse was bent over some forms.

"Quick!" I yelped, pointing back down the hall. "A cardiac arrest! He's just coming."

The nurse jumped up fast. She glanced down the hall, then grabbed the house phone and barked into it. Almost immediately I heard the calm voice of the loudspeaker saying, as smoothly as ever, "CA team to Emergency. CA team to Emergency."

That's the code used over the loudspeaker to get any available doctors to where they're needed quickly, without alarming patients. The woman in the lab coat and the nurse were already wheeling Mr. Tanner into one of the treatment rooms when I saw Dr. Vosch come hurrying along. He followed the others into the room.

I stood beside the abandoned wheelchair, my heart hammering in my ears. What had happened anyway? Had being so angry given Mr. Tanner a heart attack? And — was I going to be blamed? I was only doing my job, wheeling him to the X-ray department. Should I take the wheelchair back to Transport? Or go back to West Medical and tell them where Mr. Tanner was? Or what?

I just stood there by the wheelchair for quite a few minutes. Another nurse went into the treatment room. A few more minutes passed, and still I didn't move.

Then, just as I felt I couldn't stand it any longer, the woman in the white lab coat came out. She seemed surprised to see me still there.

"Uh — I wondered . . . " I stammered.

"Don't worry," she told me kindly. "He's going to be all right."

"Oh." That wasn't exactly what I'd been worrying about. But I gave her a half-smile and said, "Uh — that's good."

Then she went on. "And it was very alert of you to notice that he was so ill. Good work," she said, as she moved off towards the nurses' station. "Good work!"

Relief flooded over me. Nobody was going to blame me for what had happened. I gripped the handles of the wheelchair and started pushing it slowly back to the Transport room. Nothing like this had ever happened before on my candystriper days. And to think Tory had been complaining that our job was dull! All the girls will be surprised when I tell them about this, I thought.

But then, as I returned the wheelchair to its place, I thought again. I didn't feel like telling Tory about it, or the other girls either. I just wanted to keep it to myself — my own secret, my own bit of glory over those words "good work."

It made me feel special somehow. Special and important. And I liked that feeling.

3
Puppyfat

I hugged my special secret to myself for the rest of my hospital shift. I was planning to tell Mom about it at home, of course. But as soon as I opened the back door I could hear an argument in full swing.

"You're not wearing my boucle sweater and that's that," Mom was saying from the kitchen. "Your blouse looks fine now."

I saw Katie in the pink blouse, with freshly washed hair, frowning at her reflection in the hall mirror. "Did you get invited to the party after all?" I asked her.

"Yeah," she answered briefly.

"How come you're dressed so early?"

"Going to Marilyn's for supper first." She tugged at the neckline of the blouse, still frowning, and then shouted into the kitchen. "Mom! This looks dumb!"

"Katie, it does not," Mom called back.

Mom came into the hall to stand beside Katie and study her reflection too. "It looks just fine," she said again. "But if you want to change it you can tie a scarf at the neck."

"A scarf?" said Katie. "That pink silk scarf of yours?"

"Well . . . I guess you can borrow that. Just make sure it doesn't get lost. Come on upstairs and I'll help you tie it."

I could see from the two plates Mom had prepared in the kitchen that we were having a salad for supper. Mom was still taking her diet seriously. But I was hungry after my busy day so I made myself a peanut butter sandwich as well, and carried my supper down to the family room. Eating in front of the television is only allowed when Dad's away. I could hear Katie arguing about what time she had to be home — "But Mom, nobody else has to be home by eleven-thirty!" — till at last the back door closed loudly. I wondered if she was wearing Mom's boucle sweater after all. Katie usually gets whatever she wants.

After a few moments Mom's voice floated down from the kitchen. "You took your salad plate, did you Melanie?"

"Yes. And a peanut butter sandwich too."

"Okay."

Mom didn't bring her own plate down. She doesn't like my choice of programs. When I finished my supper and took my plate back upstairs she was watching the television in the living room.

"Are you going out tonight, Melanie?" she asked, one eye on the screen.

"Yes. Rhona and I are going to the early show at the Westway. I'm supposed to meet her in twenty minutes."

"Okay. Have a good time."

I noticed she didn't say anything about when I had to be home. She knew I'd come home as soon as the movie was over. What else would there be for me to do? It wasn't that I wanted an argument as I went out the door, like Katie — but a little more attention might be nice, I thought.

Rhona was waiting for me in front of the theatre. Valerie and Paul and a couple of other kids from school were there too. They were laughing loudly and talking non-stop. What do they find to say to each other all the time? I wondered. Out of the corner of my eye I watched Valerie for a while, trying to figure out just what she did that made boys fall over her so. Was it because she always acted as if she knew she was the prettiest girl around? Imagine being that sure of yourself! I guess if you felt like that you wouldn't worry about what you were saying. You'd think you could say anything at all and people would like it.

While I was still watching her, Valerie started to snuggle up to Paul and run her hand over the nape of his neck, and he responded by giving her a kiss. I turned away then. That sort of thing embarrasses me. If that's the way you had to act with a boyfriend then I didn't want one. Not that there was much chance of my getting one anyway. Would it be worse to have to act like that — or never to have a boyfriend at all? I just didn't know.

At that point the line started to move. Once we were inside Rhona and I bought our popcorn and went to choose our seats.

"Not over there!" I hissed at Rhona. "We don't want to sit by Dora."

Dora is probably the least popular girl in our class. She's really overweight and, worse than that, she smells.

"Oh, right," Rhona agreed, "we sure don't. What a dog she is. Let's sit on this side."

We took our seats and dipped into our popcorn, and then I said, "I wonder how that expression got started, anyway."

"Huh?" said Rhona, her mouth full of popcorn. "What expression?"

"Using 'dog' to mean an ugly girl."

Rhona shrugged. "I don't know. Same way that using 'nerd' for a weird-looking boy got started, I guess."

"But dogs are nice," I objected. "They're cuddly and affectionate and cute."

Rhona gave a snort. "Well, Dora Hemstead sure isn't," she said and turned her attention back to her popcorn.

The movie wasn't great. Also, Valerie and Paul sat a couple of rows ahead of us, and I couldn't help seeing how they spent the whole movie snuggling up to each other. I would've liked to move — only I didn't want to tell Rhona why. That sort of thing doesn't seem to bother Rhona.

When the movie was over I said good-bye to Rhona and headed home. Mom was still watching television when I came in.

"Hi," she called out from the living room. "Was it a good movie?"

"Not really," I called back.

I realized that I still hadn't told her about

what had happened at the hospital with Mr. Tanner, and the woman in the white lab coat saying "Good work!" But I wanted to tell her sometime when she would really listen, not while she was watching TV.

"This movie isn't bad," Mom was going on. "Fred Astaire is in it. Want to watch with me?"

"Uh, no thanks. I don't like his movies. Besides, I should work on my project some more."

"Okay," she said agreeably. "How's it going anyway?"

"Well . . . I can't get one of my drawings to look like what it's supposed to be."

"Never mind — you'll get a good mark, I'm sure. I never have to worry about your grades," she said as she turned back to Fred Astaire.

I didn't say anything about that. I suppose Mom meant it to be comforting. But at the back of my mind a little niggly voice prodded at me. "What if I don't get a good mark this time?" the little voice asked. "What if I can't keep up my good reports? What then?"

* * *

The next Friday Dad came home. Mom forgot all about diets and we had a big roast lamb dinner in the dining room. We used the good dishes and there were even flowers on the table. Mom had her hair done (she usually has it done on Fridays) and Katie and I combed ours and washed our faces. We looked like one of those happy families in a television commercial — and since Katie was in a good mood, we even sounded like one.

"So — what's new with everyone?" Dad asked after we were all served.

"I've lost some weight since you left," Mom announced proudly. (I knew that already. She'd been announcing her progress all week.) "I'd like to lose a bit more before I start trying on bathing suits."

"When I start trying on new bathing suits I want a bikini," Katie put in. "A bright red one."

"A bikini?" said Dad.

"Uh-huh," said Katie. "I'm old enough for a bikini now. And I've got the figure too."

Dad put on a look of mock surprise. "My little girl is growing up, is she? How about that? And turning into a real dish, too!"

He sounded quite delighted about that and Katie smirked happily. Perhaps it was that note of delight that made me speak up then — something I don't usually do. "What about me, Dad?" I asked him. "I'm growing up too. Am I a dish as well?"

"Well — " he answered jokingly, "you have to be good-looking — after all, everyone says how much you look like me."

That wasn't the kind of answer I was fishing for. I wanted more than just a joke. "No, really," I said again, "am I a dish too?"

"Of course you are," Dad answered, helping himself to some more roast lamb. "You have good bones in your face. When your puppyfat goes you'll be a real cutie."

"Puppyfat?" I frowned, remembering the conversation with Rhona. "Puppyfat? You mean I'm a 'dog' the way I am? That's what the boys at school call a girl who looks awful!"

"No, no, no. Of course not," Dad said quickly. "Puppyfat is just an expression. Children — and puppies — always look more . . . rounded than adults, that's all. You don't have to get upset about it."

"Oh."

I didn't say any more then. Katie went back to the subject of bikinis and Mom said she thought fifteen was too young for a really skimpy one and Katie started to argue about that — and then we didn't sound like a happy television family any more, and everyone forgot about me. But later, up in my room, I thought back to what Dad had said and stood in front of my mirror looking hard at myself.

Am I fat? I wondered. I wasn't like Dora, I was sure of that. My face is quite broad — but, as Dad said, I take after him and his face is broad too. But what about the rest of me? I studied my front view and then my side view. From the side I could see the swelling under my sweater where my bust was growing. But that didn't count as fat, did it? Surely not — why, the girls at school, and Katie too, are all proud of their growing bustlines. Even Valerie who's such a willowy type wears a bra all the time. I thought of Valerie, so tall and slim, with long blonde hair halfway down her back making her look even slimmer. I wouldn't look like her, I knew, even if I did lose some puppyfat.

Remembering that word again I scowled into the mirror. Maybe it was just an expression — but it was another slam at dogs. What does everyone have against dogs anyway? I like dogs. When I was little I often used to ask Mom whether we could have one. I would have loved a cute little dog to cuddle and talk to and take for walks. But Mom had always said no. She said dogs were hard to housebreak, and besides, they usually shed their hair all over the place and drooled. So we never did get one.

All that evening Dad's words stuck in my mind. And it was a strange thing — when I came back downstairs it seemed that everywhere I looked, all evening, I was reminded again and again about my puppyfat. On television, for instance, there were dozens of commercials for weight-watcher foods and calorie-free pop and diet frozen dinners, all supposedly guaranteed to turn you into the glamorous thin models that were in the commercials. And the magazine Mom had left on the coffee table had a front cover head-line that read *Diet desserts you can safely enjoy* and a back cover advertisement with before-and-after photographs of a woman who'd lost tons of weight by taking some kind of pills. The adver-tising business sure made a lot of money out of diets, I thought to myself.

Besides the ads, all the actresses on televi-sion reminded me of how I looked too. I'd never noticed before how skinny they all were. How did they ever get that thin? I'd read somewhere that television cameras made everyone look fatter than they really were — so those actresses all had to be super thin.

It seemed, that evening, that every woman in the world was thin or else trying to become thin. Even the television guide was full of ads for weight-loss clinics and reducing machines. *Lose weight without hunger pangs!* they said. *Burn off 800 calories an hour with our patented rowing machine! 30 days to a brand new you!*

I sat and stared at that last ad for quite a while. I'd sure like a new me, I thought to myself. Would losing some weight do it?

4
Counting calories

I still don't know whether I'd have actually done anything about that puppyfat if fate hadn't stepped in. Probably not. But it happened that the next day I got my period.

I hate having my period. I hate everything about it, it's all gross. Those girls at school who don't have theirs yet and can't wait to start — they don't realize what it's like. And they sure don't realize how much getting your period can hurt. Mom says that my cramps will become less severe when I'm older. And maybe she's right — but that weekend, even taking an aspirin and putting a hot water bottle on my stomach didn't help much.

Luckily that Saturday wasn't one of my candystriper days, so I just stayed in bed all day. Mom was cooking up a big dish of lasagna for dinner and I could smell the spicy aroma of the tomato sauce wafting up from the kitchen. But having food in my stomach always makes my cramps worse, so I wasn't planning to eat any that day.

Around lunchtime Mom brought me up some consomme.

"Feeling any better?" she asked.

"No. I took another aspirin."

"Did you? Well, don't take any more. That's enough aspirin for now."

She put the mug of consomme down on my beside table, with a coaster under it to protect the wood. Lying there, I thought back to the times when I was still little — if I was sick Mom would sometimes sit on my bed and feel my forehead, and maybe hold my hand or stroke my hair. That used to comfort me, I remembered. And I thought how comforting it would be right now.

I reached out towards her arm. "Mom," I began.

"Mmm?" said Mom.

She'd picked up the empty water glass from my table, and, after checking to see that it hadn't left a ring, she was already taking a step towards the door. "Did you want something else?" she asked briskly.

"Uh . . . no." I tucked my hand back underneath the blanket. "It's okay."

"Well, then, I'd better get back to the kitchen and stir my sauce," she went on. "That hot consomme should help you a bit. And maybe you'll feel like some supper later on."

"I don't think so," I told her, and closed my eyes again.

I could hear her footsteps going quickly back downstairs. I heard Dad's footsteps now and again too, but he didn't come in. And to tell the truth, I was just as glad. I felt embarrassed, somehow, to have him know what was wrong with me. Suppose . . . suppose I smelled? And I knew I must look a mess, with my hair all tangled and greasy.

By Sunday the cramps weren't much better. Mom made lobster Newburg for dinner, which I don't like anyway, so I stayed in bed and drank more consomme. Dad was leaving in the evening for another trip, to Texas this time. Just before he left he stuck his head in my bedroom door.

"Bye, Melanie," he said. "See you in about ten days."

"Okay, Dad," I answered.

I noticed he didn't say anything like "Hope you feel better soon." Perhaps he felt embarrassed by my ailment too. Anyway, he left, and then I got up to make sure my dirndl skirt was clean to wear to school the next day. I never wear jeans when I'm having my period; I'm too worried that something might show. I'd have to get up early enough to wash my hair before school too — it was a mess after a weekend in bed.

I wish I was a boy, I thought. Boys don't have periods. And they don't have to worry about clothes either, or hair styles, or make-up. No one expects them to look like the models on TV. Probably no one cares about their puppyfat either. It's only women that are shown in all the commercials for reducing clinics and diet pop. It'd be a lot easier to be a boy, I sighed to myself.

But the next morning when I was combing my hair in front of the mirror, I exclaimed right out loud, "Hey, look at me!" I actually looked a bit thinner after my weekend on nothing but consomme and ginger ale. Maybe wearing a long skirt helped too — but as I peered in the mirror and turned my head this way and that, it seemed to me that my face was definitely thinner. And a little pale, too. I sucked in my cheeks and put on a wan expression and struck a pose like some interestingly frail heroine in a book.

Mind you, no one at school noticed anything different about me. But with my stomach still so empty I did feel thinner. Maybe I should try to lose some of my puppyfat roundness, I thought. It wouldn't be hard to do — Mom could always lose weight when she wanted to. I thought about it all day, and as soon as I got home I went straight to the kitchen and took out all of Mom's calorie charts.

I'd never even glanced at those charts before, in spite of all Mom's chatter about calories. Now my eyes opened in amazement — because what the charts told me was staggering. Why, just a piece of bread and butter came to 170 calories, even without any peanut butter or jam on it. The toast and honey I usually had for breakfast would be lots more than that. And the ginger ale I'd been drinking all weekend was at least 100 calories a glassful. The consomme was okay, only 15 calories, but there didn't seem to be anything else very low in calories except lettuce and celery and mushrooms. And diet pop, I supposed. A cup of hot chocolate with whipped cream, on the other hand, was listed at an unbelievable 340 calories.

I sat there at the kitchen table, figuring out in my head what I normally ate in a day and how many calories that would be. It came to quite a lot. One of the charts had a photograph of a thin smiling girl on its cover. No wonder she's smiling, I thought — being that thin. I'd sure have to cut out an awful lot of foods to ever look like that.

While I was still sitting there, the phone rang. It was Dan.

"Hey, Melanie," he said (Dan seldom bothered with "Hello" or "How are you?"), "my dad found a good picture for you. For your project, I mean. Have you handed it in yet?"

"No. It's not due till Wednesday."

"Good, then you can use this. Come on over."

I put the calorie charts back in the drawer and went next door. The picture Dan's father had found was a good one. And Mr. Boucher was always pleased if you had actual photographs in your project.

"Gosh, that's great," I said to Dan. "Can I keep it?"

"Sure. It's from one of Dad's old engineering magazines."

"Thanks."

I didn't know quite what to say — he'd obviously gone to a lot of trouble for me. But Dan just answered, "That's okay. Come on downstairs and see what I've done to the new signal. I'll put on the kettle for some hot chocolate first."

Dan turned towards the stove. But the words

"hot chocolate" rang in my mind like an alarm. I could still see the figures from the calorie chart: 340 calories. Maybe even more, the way Dan made it. The figures seemed to dance in front of my eyes, bold and black.

"Uh — no thanks," I said quickly before he could reach for the kettle. "No hot chocolate for me."

Dan halted in mid-reach and turned to stare. "Huh?" he said. "Why not? We always have hot chocolate."

"Well, I was sick on the weekend. I . . . had stomach flu."

"Oh." He nodded understandingly. "Okay. Want some ginger ale instead?"

My mind raced busily through those charts, trying to remember the exact figure for ginger ale. But then the television commercials from the other night floated into my memory. "Is it diet ginger ale?" I asked.

"Diet ginger ale?" Dan turned again for another stare. "Why do you want diet stuff?"

"I . . . I like it."

"You do? I think it tastes weird. Anyway, we don't have any. My mom says those artificial sweeteners aren't good for you."

"Never mind then," I said. "I won't have anything."

"Okay."

Dan made his own hot chocolate and we went down to see how he'd landscaped the train table around the new signal. But I really didn't pay much attention to what he was showing me. All I could think of was that mug of hot chocolate he was drinking and how delicious it smelled. I almost changed my mind, right then, and asked for some. But I didn't. And after a while I began to feel terribly . . . virtuous. To want something so much and not let myself have it — that took real self-discipline, I thought. It wasn't everybody who could do that. In fact, I didn't know *anybody* else who could.

The virtuous feeling stayed with me, and after I went home I spoke to Mom in the kitchen.

"You know what, Mom," I said, "I think I'll go on a diet too."

Mom's reaction to the word diet was quite different from Dan's. "Really?" she said, sounding almost pleased.

"Yeah. You know — lose that puppyfat Dad was talking about."

"Well, you're not fat — but everybody looks better a little bit lighter, I think."

"Yeah," I agreed. "What's for supper tonight, anyway?"

"Oh, nothing fancy tonight. Just some chicken from last week, with mashed potatoes and green beans. A pretty good diet meal, except for the potatoes."

"No potatoes for me then," I said.

"Okay. Any gravy?"

"No. Just chicken and green beans."

I placed my order glibly. But by this time my cramps had disappeared and I was really hungry. It was hard, harder than I'd expected, to pass up the potatoes and gravy. The chicken and beans looked awfully skimpy on my plate — so to make it seem like more, I spent the first few minutes at the table arranging my supper carefully: the slices of meat overlapping exactly, the green beans in a perfect circle. And then I ate my meal in an exact pattern too: one small mouthful of chicken, one green bean. That helped take my mind off how hungry I was, and how much Katie was eating. One bite of chicken and one bean, very slowly, mouthful after mouthful.

And it worked, for most of the meal. But then Katie brought some leftover apple pie to the table. It had been heating in the oven and it smelled spicy and delicious.

"Oh, that smells good," Mom exclaimed. "I think I'll cheat on my diet and have a tiny piece."

"Okay," said Katie, cutting off a thin wedge for her. "And I'll divide the rest in half. I divide and you choose — that's fair," she said to me.

"Uh — no," I said quickly.

Katie flared up immediately. "What do you mean, no? It is so fair!"

"No — I mean I don't want any pie."

"You don't? Oh." She calmed down again. "That's different. You still sick or something?"

"No, she's not sick," Mom put in. "Melanie has decided to join me and start dieting too."

"Dieting? Her too?" Katie sounded scornful. "Well, you won't catch me joining you. Hey — does that mean I can have as big a piece as I want?

"I guess so," answered Mom.

I left the table quickly. But even up in my room I could smell that hot spicy pie. I could always change my mind and have a small piece, I thought. After all, Mom was having some. Apple pie was about 300 calories a slice, I remembered, so a third of a normal slice would only be about 100 calories . . .

But again, I didn't change my mind. If I was going to diet I'd do it properly, the way it was supposed to be done — which meant no dessert, not even a small piece. And as I sat at my desk that virtuous feeling crept over me once more. It didn't make my half-empty stomach any more comfortable, but it made me feel quite different. I felt special, the way I had at the hospital that day. And superior too. I was better at dieting than even Mom, I thought, and I'd only just started. I was disciplined, disciplined and . . . pure. Perhaps even saintly — "mortifying the flesh" was just what I was doing, wasn't it?

I stayed in my room all that evening, partly because I didn't trust myself to go near the kitchen. But mostly it was to hug that special feeling to myself. It was wonderful to feel better than everyone else. It was worth an empty rumbling stomach.

*   *   *

For the rest of that week I sat in the kitchen after school every day, studying Mom's calorie charts. And since I'm good at memorizing, it wasn't long before I had most of the figures fixed firmly in my mind. Maybe even too firmly — I soon found that every time I looked around the lunchroom and saw somebody's candy bar or cupcake or brownie, the number of calories they contained would seem to hover in front of my eyes. How could they eat that fattening stuff? I wondered. Didn't they know?

The number of calories in my own lunch — and breakfast and supper — was never far from my mind either. But that number was pretty low. There was no more honey and toast for me at breakfast, no peanut butter and banana sandwiches in my lunch, no dessert at supper. No dessert at all. I think I began to make Mom feel a bit guilty when I kept turning it down every single night.

"It's all right to have a little ice cream now and again, Melanie," she would tell me as she served herself a small dishful.

But I didn't have any. If I'm going to do something, I want to do it as perfectly as I can. Being on a diet means no dessert, and that's that. And it all seemed worthwhile when, a week later on my next candystriper Saturday, somebody did notice a difference in me.

"Why, Melanie, have you been losing weight?" Mrs. Sullivan asked as I hung up my jacket in the candystripers' room.

"Uh — yes. I have."

"My goodness, aren't you wonderful!" she exclaimed. "I wish I could lose some. I try, but I can never stay on a diet. I just like food too much, you see."

I didn't say anything to that. But I couldn't quite hide a scornful look at her words. Did she think I didn't like food? Did she think it was easy to come in after school, starved, and just go up to my room? Did she think it was easy to smell Katie's frozen waffles in the toaster and not have one myself?

But I was better than she was, I reminded myself. I was disciplined. I cast a quick glance at her rounded stomach — which her tight slacks made very visible — and suddenly I didn't mind the gnawing sensation that was in my stomach most of the time now. I was even proud of it as I lifted my head high and walked away.

That Saturday was quite busy. For the first hour I stayed in the candystripers' room to answer the telephone. There are always magazines lying around there and one of them caught my eye. The model on the cover looked a little like Valerie Novak from school. She had long blonde hair like Valerie, but she was thinner, a lot thinner.

That's how thin I'd like to be, I thought to myself. Maybe I should let my own hair grow long like hers. If Mom would let me, that is — she usually hauls me off to her hairdresser the minute my bangs begin to get shaggy. Mom would probably say that long hair looks messy.

All the same I tucked the magazine into my knapsack to take home with me. I'd cut that picture out, I decided. She could be my inspiration, my goal. I'd love to look like her.

After the first hour by the telephone I was put on flower delivery. There were a lot of flowers and I walked miles. I kept a sharp lookout for the doctor who'd helped me on my last candystriper day — the young one with the long dark hair — but I didn't see her. By lunchtime I was tired, and very hungry.

"Oh, good!" said Bitsy, who was in line behind me. "Lasagna today. I hope I get a big serving."

I didn't answer. I was busy studying the salad plates, trying to calculate how many calories each one had. Bitsy noticed where I was standing.

"You're not going to have a salad, are you?" she asked. "Gee — the lasagna is the best meal they have here."

It was, too. Not as delicious as Mom's, but good. "Uh, no," I answered. "Not today. I . . . just feel like a salad."

"You haven't got your dessert," Bitsy went on, staring down at my tray. "And we've already passed the dessert section."

"I know. I'll . . . maybe get one later if I'm still hungry."

"But — " Bitsy was still frowning at my tray, "but you have to hand in your lunch ticket now. If you go back for dessert later you'll have to pay."

"Then I'll pay!" I told her angrily. "Just leave me to choose my own lunch, will you?"

I picked out a salad plate with cottage cheese and a diet pop, and handed my lunch ticket to the cashier. It wasn't very much lunch, but I could manage on that. I walked quickly to a corner of the cafeteria and sat down by myself, away from the other candystripers — and away from the smell of their darned lasagna. Besides, I needed to sit by myself so I could decide how to arrange my plate. Arranging my food in a pattern on the plate and then eating it to a pattern made it easier to forget how little I was eating. So now I divided each item on my plate into four: four piles of cottage cheese, four pieces of celery, four wedges of hard-boiled egg, four piles of lettuce. Then I ate one mouthful from each pile, in strict order — and when I'd finished I hardly noticed that I was still hungry.

My stomach noticed it, though. By two o'clock I was feeling sort of dizzy. I sat down by the phone in the candystripers' room and put my head on my arms for a moment to see if that might help.

"What's wrong, Melanie?" Mrs. Sullivan asked.

"I . . . I'm a bit dizzy," I explained, quite truthfully. And then I went on less truthfully. "I had stomach flu last week."

"Did you? Well then, just sit there and answer the phone. Bitsy and Jane — you go to Surgical, second floor. I'm needed in Admitting."

I was glad to sit there by the phone. And I was glad to be alone too. I didn't feel like talking to anybody, not even Bitsy. Somehow, candystriping didn't seem very enjoyable that day.

5

Birthday blues

When I got home, Dad was there. He'd arrived in from Texas a few hours earlier. As soon as he saw me he gave a whistle.

"Hey! Look at you, Melanie! Mom told me you'd joined her on a diet. You've really lost some weight."

"Yeah," I answered, pleased that he'd noticed. "I have."

"Looks great on you!"

My spirits lifted right away at his admiring tone. It wasn't often that he told me anything like that. But Katie soon horned in on the conversation.

"Hunh!" she scoffed, "you wouldn't catch me dieting! Boys don't like girls that are too skinny. They like some curves."

"I don't care what boys like," I said.

Katie stared. "Then why are you dieting?"

"For myself," I told her. "Just for me, myself. Because I want to be thin."

"Hunh!" she said again, and rolled her eyes in disbelief.

For dinner that night Mom had made turkey tetrazzini. I couldn't remember seeing that in any of her calorie charts, but I knew it had noodles and cream and sherry and goodness knows what else in it, so it sure had to be fattening. I sniffed longingly. I was hungry. But as Mom was serving, Dad smiled at me and said, "Not too much of this rich concoction for our dieters, I guess."

And then it was easy to smile back and say, "No, not too much for me, please."

Mind you, Dad did drop his smile a couple of times during dinner to say sharply, "Melanie, don't play with your food like that." Only I wasn't playing with it. I was just arranging it, making sure the turkey and the salad didn't touch each other so I could take alternate mouthfuls. I had to do that, no matter what Dad said. Sometimes I counted my mouthfuls too, so I wasn't paying much attention to the conversation at the table. But at one point Katie caught my interest.

"Hey, Mom," she said, "I watched *Gone With The Wind* on the Simmons' VCR last night. And I got to thinking — Scarlett O'Hara was actually

Katie Scarlett, you know. And her rival was Melanie, Melanie Wilkes. Did you name us after the movie? Is that where you got our names?"

Mom's eyes took on a misty air. *"Gone With The Wind* . . . Oh, how I loved that movie. I must've seen it at least five times."

"And is that why you named us Katie and Melanie?" Katie asked again.

"No," said Mom, still misty-eyed. "As a matter of fact I'd quite forgotten that Scarlett was actually Katie Scarlett."

"So had I," said Dad. "But if we had named you two after the movie, we certainly gave the right name to the right daughter: quiet well-behaved Melanie and rambunctious noisy Katie."

"Yeah!" said Katie, not a bit offended. "I'm glad I'm rambunctious like Scarlett. Scarlett had more fun. Besides, I don't want to be quiet and good like Melanie Wilkes and end up dying young."

"Oh, I don't think our Melanie is going to die young," said Dad. "In fact you have a birthday coming up soon, don't you, Melanie? Turning thirteen?"

"Not thirteen!" I looked up from my plate, stung into speech. Didn't Dad even know how old I was? "I'm going to be fourteen!"

"Fourteen!" Dad raised his eyebrows in exaggerated surprise. "Why, soon you two will be grown up and wanting to get married! I'd better start saving for your weddings."

"You sure better," Katie agreed. "I'm going to have a huge one!"

"You would," said Dad, laughing. Then he turned back to me. "How many are coming to your party, Melanie? Are you inviting some boys this year?"

"That's just what I've been asking her, too," Mom put in. "Melanie says she doesn't want a party."

"No party?" said Dad. "Of course you want a party! Don't you, Melanie?"

"Uh — well, I haven't decided yet," I answered quickly. "I'll . . . I'll think about it. I don't know who I want to invite yet."

"You'll have to decide soon. Your birthday is next Friday," Mom pointed out.

"I know," I said, and turned my attention back to counting mouthfuls.

As soon as I could, I excused myself from the table. The fact that I wasn't having dessert gave me a good excuse to leave. I carried my empty plate to the kitchen and hurried back up to my room.

I wish it wasn't my fourteenth birthday! I thought as I plunked myself down in front of my dresser. I wish I was turning four instead, with nobody talking about growing up and having mixed parties and getting married. I didn't want to grow up; it would be much nicer to stay thirteen and never have to worry about boyfriends and dating. It would be even nicer to still be twelve and not have to worry about periods either. Twelve would be just great, for ever and ever.

But that couldn't happen, of course. I sat at my dresser and peered into my pretty gilt-edged mirror to see whether my face was looking any thinner. It seemed to me it was. And paler, too. I actually do look a little like the Melanie in *Gone With The Wind*, I thought. At least I would if my hair was parted in the middle the way hers was. I picked up my comb and tried parting it like that. My bangs were a problem though. I had to pin them back with bobby pins to keep the part in place — and that didn't look at all like Melanie Wilkes' soft dark wings of hair.

Disappointed, I threw down my comb. Besides, I thought, Katie was right — Melanie Wilkes didn't have much fun in the movie. She just stayed home being good, instead of going to parties. And what was I going to do about my party? I didn't want one. I'd feel stupid asking a bunch of kids from my class to a party when they aren't even my friends. All I really wanted on my birthday was to have my locker decorated.

I leaned forward on my elbows and let myself picture the scene. I'd turn down the hallway, sauntering along casually — and then I'd suddenly catch sight of a flash of bright color ahead. And I'd see Rhona standing by my locker. And maybe Monica and Sandy — they sometimes eat lunch with Rhona and me, so they could be standing around too. They wouldn't mind doing that. And I'd be so surprised — really surprised, not just putting it on like Valerie did. And I wouldn't show off the way she did. I'd just look pleased, and they'd all say "Happy birthday, Melanie!" In grade school the whole class used to sing "Happy Birthday" to me because Mom used to bake cupcakes and bring them over to school for the teacher to give out at recess. Mom used to let me dress up for school on my birthday too, and everyone would ooh and aah over the huge tray of cupcakes, and I'd feel so wonderful, so special.

It would be great to feel that way again.

* * *

Of course, real life hardly ever turns out the same as daydreams. And my birthday sure didn't. When I got to school that Friday I did saunter down the hallway, casual and nonchalant. I just couldn't help hoping that maybe, just maybe . . .

But one glance towards my row of lockers punctured those hopes. There was no flash of brightly colored paper and no group of waiting friends. Just gray locker doors. Gray, gray, gray.

Rhona was already there.

"Hi," she said briefly. Her head was half inside her locker as she searched through the pile of junk for her books.

I didn't answer. I was too crushed to speak.

"Oh, hey," Rhona went on, "I almost forgot — happy birthday."

I bent over the books in my own locker, not to find anything but to hide my face. I mustn't cry, I thought. I mustn't.

Beside me Rhona slammed her door. "What's wrong?" she asked. "It is your birthday today, isn't it? Today's the day you've invited me to dinner?"

I managed to find my voice. "Yeah, it's today."

"I thought it was. So — happy birthday."

"Yeah, thanks," I muttered, pulling my

books out quickly. "Come on, hurry up. We'll be late."

We were nowhere near being late; the first bell hadn't even rung yet. But I headed off toward our home room without waiting for Rhona. When I got there the room was still empty except for a few girls at the back of the room and our teacher, Mrs. Rivera.

I went to my desk and dropped my books more noisily than I usually did. At the clatter Mrs. Rivera looked up.

"Melanie," she said, "I've noticed something different about you. You've lost weight, haven't you?"

I paused, halfway into my seat. "Uh, yes," I said.

"You're not sick, are you?"

"No. Of course not. I'm just dieting, that's all."

One of the girls at the back of the room spoke up. "Are you?" she said. "You really look different, Melanie."

"I do?" I couldn't hide my surprise. Or my pleasure. I didn't think anyone besides Rhona ever noticed me at all.

"Yes, you do," Mrs. Rivera agreed. "That's why I wondered if you were all right."

"I'm fine," I told her. "Just fine."

The first bell rang and the room began to fill up. I sat down and spread open my books to get ready for class, just as I always did. But inside I was bubbling over. People are beginning to notice, I thought. I look different already! Just wait till I'm as thin as the girl on that magazine cover. Then I'll really be noticed. I'll be noticed as much as Valerie is. When I'm thin like that, everyone will really admire me. And like me too. I'll be popular. Just wait, I thought. Just wait!

*   *   *

As Rhona had mentioned at school, she was coming to dinner that night. I'd finally convinced Mom that I didn't want a party, that I'd rather have a couple of friends for dinner and go to a movie afterwards. And I'd actually screwed up enough courage to ask Monica and Sandy too. Only they were competing in a swim meet that night. At least they said they were. And maybe they actually were busy — but it still left just Rhona coming for my "party."

I was glad that Dad wasn't home; he'd have made a fuss. Perhaps Mom was disappointed in me too, but she didn't say anything. She had the table nicely set in the dining room for the four of us. And she'd cooked roast beef as I'd asked. I didn't want anything fattening like lasagna or spaghetti.

Rhona knew I was dieting, of course, since we ate lunch together. But even so her eyebrows went up when I didn't take anything but roast beef and salad on my plate.

"How can you pass up these yummy roast potatoes?" she asked, helping herself to a pile of them.

I gave a noncommittal shrug and said nothing.

"I don't know why you want to lose weight, anyway," Rhona went on.

"Why?" I repeated. "Why? What a dumb question! Everybody wants to lose weight."

"I don't," said Katie. "I'm never going to diet."

"Oh — you will someday," Mom put in. "Wait till you're my age. Most women have to start dieting sooner or later."

"They do?" said Rhona, still sounding unconvinced.

"Well, sure," I told her. "Just look at any magazine. They're full of ads for reducing clinics and low-cal foods and diet pop, and full of articles on how to lose weight. And not just for women —

for girls too. All the models you see are really thin."

"They are?" said Rhona. "I never noticed."

I shot her a disgusted glance to show her how stupid she was being. I'd quite forgotten that I hadn't noticed either, not till that evening when Dad had started talking about puppyfat. I stayed annoyed with her, not talking much, for the rest of the first course. But then — then Mom brought in the birthday cake.

It was square, with white icing and yellow and pink roses in each corner, and pink writing that said *Happy Birthday, Melanie*. Mom had bought it at a fancy bakery and had put it on our best silver cake plate.

"I just bought a small cake this year," Mom was saying. "I remember last year at your party we had the double size and still there was squabbling about who would get the icing roses."

"Can I have a rose this year?" Rhona asked quickly.

"And me," said Katie. "I want a corner piece."

"Our guest should have the corner piece," Mom told Katie reprovingly, "and our birthday girl."

"Well, there are four corners and four people," answered Katie, "so why can't we each have a corner piece?"

"Oh Katie, you can't cut a cake like that."

I was scarcely listening to the conversation — I was in a panic. I hadn't planned ahead properly. What was I going to do about this cake? There had to be a zillion calories in a cake like this! One big piece of that gooey confection would put all my lost weight right back on.

"You cut, Melanie," said Mom, handing me the knife. "And don't forget to make a wish."

I was too busy panicking to make a proper wish. I just said to myself, "I want to be really thin," and plunged the knife in. I cut a big corner piece for Rhona and one for Katie, then an edge piece for Mom ("Not too big a piece for me, Melanie," Mom said) and then cut a small inside piece for myself. That brought another outburst from Rhona.

"Is that all you're having?" Her face was a picture of disbelief.

"Well, I am on a diet, you know," I snapped.

"I know. But it's your birthday cake! One piece of cake won't make any difference."

While I shot her another angry glare Mom leapt in to change the subject. I'd probably get a lecture from her later, I realized, about being polite to guests. But I didn't care. As I pushed my sliver of cake around the plate, nibbling a few crumbs and carefully avoiding the gooey icing, I wished I'd never invited Rhona in the first place. Didn't she realize that if I ate one big piece of cake I might want more? Want it so much that I wouldn't be able to stop myself? It might taste so good that I'd just lose control over myself completely, and eat and eat and eat . . .

* * *

It was later that night, after I'd come home from the movie, that Mom spoke to me. Only it wasn't about manners after all.

"Melanie," she said, "I think you're going at your diet a bit too strenuously. You didn't really eat any of your cake — your very own birthday cake."

"I ate some of it!" I protested.

"About a mouthful, that's all. When I cleared the plates away I could see most of it still there under your crumpled napkin." She frowned. "You were never actually fat, Melanie. I think you've lost enough weight now."

"Oh, I haven't lost enough yet!"

"I think you have. You've lost quite a lot, you know."

70

"I know," I said proudly. "But I want to lose a little bit more — for insurance, sort of. You've said yourself how easy it is to put weight back on as soon as you go off a diet."

"Well, yes. But you need more nourishment than you're getting now. You're still a growing girl."

"Yeah — but I don't want to grow out. I wish I'd hurry up and grow taller though. Tall girls always look thinner."

"You look thin enough already. In fact your face is quite drawn. You — "

Just then the back door burst open and Katie rushed in.

"Hey, Mom!" she said, breezing through the kitchen towards the living room. "I'm just going to get our cartridge, okay?"

Mom leapt to her feet and ran to block her way. "Wait a minute, Katie. What do you mean?"

"I'm just going to take the cartridge and needle from our stereo over to the Simmons'. We're having a dance and stupid Richard dropped the tone arm on their set."

"Katie!" Mom spread herself across the living room doorway. "You are not taking the cartridge out of your father's stereo — and that's that!"

"Oh, Mom!" wailed Katie. "We need it!"

"And what have you been eating anyway?" Mom asked her. "You've had something you shouldn't have, I can tell from the way you're acting."

"I haven't eaten anything!" Katie stormed, stamping her foot.

"What have you had to drink, then?"

"Nothing! Just a bit of pop."

"Orange pop, I suppose. Katie, you know what that does to you. You'd better try and calm down a minute before you go back."

I slipped away from the kitchen and up to my room. For once I was glad about one of Katie's outbursts — Mom would probably have forgotten all about my face by now. Besides, it wasn't drawn. It wasn't even thin enough yet. I'd have to be lots thinner than I was now to be noticed by everyone. To be noticed and popular.

6
Lunch patterns

The next morning when I looked in the refrigerator the rest of the cake was there, still on the good silver plate. In spite of Rhona's and Katie's big pieces there was a lot left. Too much — I wasn't sure I could resist all that temptation. So I cut off a large section, wrapped it in some foil, and took it next door.

"Hey," said Dan as he opened the door, "I haven't seen you in ages. Where've you been?"

"Well . . . I've been busy with homework most evenings."

"You have? How come you have so much homework? You never used to."

I shrugged. It wasn't exactly that I had more homework, it just seemed to take me all evening to get it done. I was finding it hard to concentrate. I couldn't remember things — I'd look up a word of French vocabulary and then forget it two minutes later. But I didn't tell Dan that. Instead I held out the foil-wrapped package.

"Anyway," I said, "I'm here now, and I brought some of my birthday cake for you."

"Hey, happy birthday! When was it?"

"Yesterday."

Dan unwrapped the foil eagerly. "Looks delicious," he announced. "Come on in — we'll put a candle on it and you can make another wish. I'll get some plates."

"Oh, no — I can't, Dan. I . . . have to go out. I just wanted you to have some, that's all."

"You can't come in long enough to eat a piece of cake?"

"No — really — I have to go somewhere with my Mom."

"Oh."

He didn't say anything more. But his face took on a strange look. It became suddenly blank, as if he'd closed it off from me, and though I left then — as I'd said I had to — that bothered me. It bothered me a lot. Did Dan know I was lying about having to go out? Probably; I hadn't sounded very convincing. I should've thought ahead and had a better excuse ready. Would he maybe watch to see whether Mom and I actually did go out? Should I ask Mom to take me to the store in case he did?

It really upset me to think of Dan mad at me. But I couldn't have sat down with him and eaten a whole piece of that rich gooey cake. I couldn't, that was all.

I went back up to my room and stood in front of my mirror. I was thinner, I knew that. But I still didn't look like the girl on the magazine cover, the one with the long blonde hair. I took the magazine out of my desk drawer where I kept it, and propped it up against the mirror. Standing sideways made me look even thinner, I decided. And my arm, when I stretched it out taut — that was thin. I stood with my arm held in front of me, swiveling it this way and that, finding its thinnest aspect and reveling in it. If I held my arm just so . . . and held my fingers just so . . . it could almost be a ballet dancer's arm, I thought. And that was worth having anybody mad at me, almost.

After a while I turned from the mirror and sat down at my desk. My French homework was spread out, and I picked up my pen and stared at it. But all I could see was the cake plate in the refrigerator with the rest of my birthday cake on it. Even after giving a chunk to Dan there was still a big piece left. I could picture it exactly: right down to the tail end of *rthday* in pink writing, the yellow rose in the corner, the smear of icing on the plate that outlined where the rest of the cake had been. I could smell it too, sweet and creamy. I could almost taste it.

I sat and thought about that cake for most of the morning. I found I was thinking about food a lot. About pieces of toast with loads of butter and honey, cut into fingers; about a plateful of creamy mashed potatoes topped with rich brown gravy; about crunchy cookies, and milk shakes, and ice cream, and peanut butter, and spaghetti and hot chocolate.

I never used to think about food all the time. So what did I think about before? About school, I guess — what marks I'd get, and what sort of comments I'd have on my report card, and why Valerie was so popular, and how I could be popular, and whether that group of girls in the changing room had noticed I had my period and were talking about me, and whether I'd ever have a boyfriend, and whether I wanted one anyway . . .

Just thinking about food was easier, I guess.

*   *   *

After the episode of the birthday cake I started to get cagey with Mom.

Because I didn't want any more nagging, I worked out a whole series of dodges to make her think I was eating. At breakfast, for instance, I would fix myself a bowlful of cereal and nibble at it slowly — and then as soon as Mom left the kitchen for any reason I'd dump the rest of it in the garbage. I'd take the lunch she packed for me without any argument and just throw out the sandwich, and after school I'd let her see me taking milk and cookies up to my room — and then I'd quietly get rid of them down the toilet. Supper was harder, to be sure. But since Mom was still dieting to get into her size 10 bathing suit she couldn't say too much to me, especially if she thought I'd had milk and cookies after school.

During the next few weeks I got quite good at being cagey like that. And luckily for me Mom had a lot on her mind right then. She'd decided the family room needed to be done over, with a real fireplace put in. (I don't really know why, since our furnace keeps the whole house warm enough.) That turned out to be a big messy job, with workmen tramping dust and dirt through the house for days and days — so that even during the week or so that Dad was home she didn't fuss with fancy dinners. Just once, on the night before Dad left on another trip, did she cook a big dinner. And that night I faked an invitation over to Rhona's and went to a movie by myself, and got out of dinner that way.

By that time, any invitation to Rhona's would have to be fake. I wasn't seeing much of her anymore. I didn't eat lunch with her; I was tired of hearing her make dumb remarks about my diet. Instead, I usually took my lunch (the part of it that I did eat: the carrot sticks and orange) outside to the hill behind the playing field. A lot of kids ate lunch outside when the weather was warm and from the hill I could watch them talking among themselves, laughing and rough-housing and flirting. And the odd thing was, I didn't have any desire to be part of them anymore. I watched them the way I might watch a play, a play I wasn't much interested in. I'd never felt I belonged to any group anyway. Now I didn't even want to. It was easier to sit up there on the hill, in a little cocoon of my own, and just look on.

As the days went by I found that my stomach didn't hurt as much either. When I'd first started to diet the gnawing hunger pains had been awful. So awful that I'd nearly given in, several times.

But after a while I scarcely noticed them. My stomach had realized that I was in control, I guess. And I liked to be alone to eat, the way I was up on the hill. When I was alone like that I could spend as long as I wanted arranging my orange sections in one pattern, my carrot sticks in another pattern, without anyone getting cross or making sarcastic remarks. I'd like to have eaten all my meals up there. Only — once or twice I found myself coming to, out of a kind of daze, and realizing that I'd spent most of the lunch hour arranging and rearranging orange sections on my lunch bag. Without even eating any. That felt a bit spooky. I couldn't help wondering how I could spend the whole period doing that. And why I felt I had to. Because even after I became aware of what I was doing, I couldn't make myself stop. I went on arranging and rearranging, right up until the bell rang for the end of the lunch period and I went in.

* * *

On my candystriping days I always wore the same white blouse, a cotton one that was open at the neck. But one hospital Saturday, some weeks after my birthday, as I was reaching for it in the closet I hesitated. I'd been wearing sweaters to school everyday — for some reason I always felt chilly. Spring didn't seem nearly as warm as normal. I debated between my usual blouse and a sweater for quite a while — for so long, in fact, that I didn't leave myself time to tidy up my room properly before I left. But at last I put on my white shaker-stitch sweater and took the blouse along in my knapsack. That way I could change if the hospital was too hot.

I shouldn't have worried; the hospital wasn't too hot. Perhaps they aren't keeping it as warm any more, I thought. But Tory was complaining.

"How can you wear a sweater in here?" she asked me. "It's stifling! Aren't you hot?"

"No," I answered. "I'm just right."

"You are? You must be peculiar."

She gave me a skeptical look as she rolled up her own shirt sleeves a little further. I turned and walked off to the flower room. I didn't want to work with her all day — I'd expected her to have dropped out of candystriping by now. So I looked around quickly for something to do. There were no flowers waiting but there was a card, addressed to someone in room 232, and I picked it up and hurried off.

I was halfway down the hallway when I remembered I hadn't checked the name against the patient file. But I didn't want to go back and encounter Tory again. So I hurried on.

Room 232 is in the children's ward on the second floor. I like the children's ward. The hallway is decorated with a Disney mural, and every room has bright curtains and clown-patterned wallpaper. Room 232, when I reached it, had two beds in it but only one was occupied — the children's wing is the one place in the hospital that's never overcrowded. That's because a lot of parents prefer the big children's hospital downtown.

The bed by the window in 232 held a little boy, about six maybe, with a freckled face. He didn't look very sick but he looked stubborn. A nurse was standing by the bed with a bottle and a spoon and there was obviously a battle going on.

"Hi, there," I said brightly. By the look of things I figured I could really be a help. "I've got something for you."

"You have?" said the boy. "What?"

"Swallow your medicine, and then I'll show you," I answered.

The boy stuck out his lower lip as if he was planning to argue some more. But after a few seconds he changed his mind. He opened his mouth, swallowed the spoonful of yellow liquid that the nurse was holding out, and then stuck out his hand to me.

"Gimme!" he said.

I held out the square envelope. "Your name's Joseph, right? Joseph Wallace?"

The little boy frowned. "I'm not Joseph," he said scornfully.

At that the nurse stepped forward and intercepted the envelope. She glanced at the address and frowned too. "This says room 282," she told me.

I came closer and stared down at the envelope in her hand. "It . . . it does?" I stammered. "Oh. It . . . it looked like 232 to me."

"Besides," the nurse went on, "you're supposed to take any delivery for the children's ward to the nursing station first, before coming to the patient's room. Hasn't anyone told you that?"

By now the little boy had started to yell. "I want my letter! You said if I took that yucky stuff I'd get something. I want it! It's mine!"

"Hush, Billy," the nurse told him. "I'm sorry, it was a mistake. The girl brought it to the wrong room."

"But I want it! I want it!" he screamed.

The nurse gave me an angry wave of her hand. "Just leave," she muttered at me. "And be more careful next time," she added, as she turned back to the crying Billy.

With my cheeks aflame, I left. How could I have been so stupid? Even if it did look like 232, I knew that on the children's ward I was supposed to take everything to the nurses' station first. I'd never made a mistake like that before. I'd never made any mistakes! I didn't *make* mistakes!

I hurried along the hall, face burning with shame, to the next ward and Room 282. I scarcely looked at Joseph Wallace (in his eighties, at least) as I handed him his card, and I didn't wait for any thanks. The nurse's words echoed over and over in my ears: "be more careful next time." Me, Melanie — I was always careful! Didn't she know that? I was Mrs. Sullivan's best candystriper! The writing wasn't very clear — and anyway, she didn't have to talk to me like that! After all, I was a volunteer, I didn't have to do this job. Maybe I won't! I thought suddenly. Maybe I'll give it up. That way I'll have more time for homework. Who needs this silly job anyway?

I headed slowly back to the candystripers' room, taking as long as I could to let my cheeks stop burning first. As I stepped out of the elevator on the main floor I saw Dr. Vosch waiting at the other bank of elevators. I hadn't seen him here at the hospital for weeks, not since that day with Mr. Tanner. Well, at least here's somebody who likes me, I thought gratefully, and managed to put on a smile.

"Hello, Dr. Vosch," I called over to him.

He glanced up, and smiled back at me. "Hello, Mel— "

But he stopped, in midsentence. His glance sharpened. "Melanie!" he said, stepping closer and putting a hand on my arm. "Have you been sick? Why have you lost so much weight?"

Out of the corner of my eye I could see a young nurse from the elevator turn and look at me. I stood up a little straighter.

"I'm all right," I answered. "I've just been dieting a bit, that's all," I went on proudly.

"A bit?" he snapped, his eyes scanning me from head to toe. "More than a bit. You come with me."

He turned sharply and led the way into the back door of Emergency. Startled, and quite puzzled, I followed. Why was he taking me into Emerg? Did he want my help for something? Perhaps that was it — only he sounded so cross.

Dr. Vosch led me down the hallway of Emergency, past the waiting patients, and into one of the treatment rooms. There was no one else there. He crossed the room and stood by a scale in the corner. "Take off your shoes," he ordered, "and climb onto that scale."

He looked stern, sterner than I'd ever seen him. Without a word I did as he said. He slid the weight along the weighing arm, then slid it back, and back some more, his face growing darker with every move. Then he turned and glared at me.

"Now, Melanie," he said, "just what do you think you're doing? You know very well that you've lost too much weight since I last saw you — don't you?"

I didn't know any such thing — but I was afraid to say so when he looked so angry. He didn't give me a chance to answer anyway.

"And just look at what you're wearing," he went on, plucking at the sleeve of my sweater. "You've lost so much weight that you can't even maintain body heat properly — otherwise you couldn't stand wearing that heavy sweater in this hot-box of a hospital. What are your parents thinking of, anyway, to let you lose so much? I'm going to phone your mother right now and set up an appointment for you in my office next week. And no more weight off, young lady! You start eating better again — do you hear me?"

I could hardly help but hear him, he was talking so angrily. Everyone out in the hallway had probably heard him too, so when he'd left I waited in the treatment room for a bit before slinking back to the candystripers' room. *Drat, drat, drat!* I thought to myself. Why did I have to bump into him today? I wish I'd never started candystriping at all!

I hurried along the hall, angry thoughts churning through my mind. Why should Dr. Vosch get so mad anyway, just because I'd lost some weight? This wasn't the way things were supposed to happen — this was nothing like the daydreams I spun for myself, about how people would notice me and admire me when I was thin. Dr. Vosch had noticed me all right, but he sure didn't sound admiring.

When I got back to the candystripers' room Bitsy was by the phone. I slumped down in one of the chairs without a word.

"They need somebody on West Medical with a wheelchair," Bitsy told me. "Do you want to go, Melanie?"

"No," I muttered. "I'm not going. I'm not going anywhere. I just may quit this whole job."

I propped my elbow on the chair arm and turned away from her, leaning my face into my hand. I sat there for quite a while, trying to shut out the memory of the nurse's voice, of Dr. Vosch's angry eyes, and of Bitsy's puzzled face.

7

The battles begin

If my dieting had posed problems with Mom before, it was nothing compared to what happened now. Dr. Vosch must have phoned her right away — because she was waiting at the door for me when I got home from the hospital.

"Melanie!" she said, her lips tight with anger, "I told you weeks ago that you were getting too thin. But you haven't paid any attention, have you?"

"I have so!" I answered. "You've seen me eating."

"Not enough," Mom said grimly. "This silly dieting has got to stop."

"Silly dieting?" I cried. "What do you mean, silly? How come it's not silly when you're doing it?"

"Because I don't make myself sick with it, that's why."

"I'm not sick."

"You will be. Dr. Vosch says so. He's made an appointment for us to see him on Tuesday, and he says you *must* gain some weight back by then."

"But I can't! I'll get fat again!"

"Melanie, I have supper ready and you're to sit down and eat it right now."

She'd made macaroni and cheese casserole, hot and bubbly, with a crispy crumb topping. She knew it was one of my favorites. But all I could see was the figure from her calorie charts, written in big black type in front of my eyes: macaroni and cheese, 300 calories per serving. And Mom had filled my plate with at least a double serving.

"Mom!" I wailed, "I can't eat all that! I can't! My stomach won't hold it. You know how a stomach can shrink!"

"You have to," she ordered.

"I *can't!*"

With a start I realized I had shrieked those words. I never shriek like that. It's Katie who always does the screaming in our house. But I couldn't eat a whole plateful of macaroni and cheese, even if I'd wanted to. I just couldn't.

There was part of me that did want to. When, with Mom's eyes fixed on me, I started nibbling at the mound of hot savory macaroni, it tasted delicious. But the other part of me was stiff with horror. Inside of me a voice was screaming, *No! You mustn't get fat! You must be the thinnest one! You must!*

With Mom standing over me I did eat some of the huge serving. She wouldn't let me divide it into four piles on my plate, the way I wanted to, and every time I put my fork down she would say, "You have to finish it, Melanie" and I would wail, "I can't" and she would say, "You have to." Finally I couldn't stand it any more. I jumped up from the table and ran upstairs to my room and slammed the door (I'm not the usual door-slammer in our house either) and cried and cried and cried. I felt so awful. My stomach hurt, with all that starchy food in it. But far worse than that was the feeling of being no longer special, no longer better than everyone else. No longer pure.

* * *

That meal set the pattern for the next three days. It was dreadful. The only thing the least bit enjoyable about that whole time was the look on Katie's face at mealtimes as Mom and I battled away. Katie wasn't used to sitting and listening to someone else's battles, or to being ignored. She would eye me strangely, almost warily, and say nothing at all.

On Monday morning Mom packed me a big lunch with two peanut butter sandwiches and a banana and a package of cookies. I looked at it aghast.

"You've got to eat it, Melanie," she told me. "I'll call Rhona tonight and ask her whether you ate it all or not."

"We don't have the same lunch hour any more," I lied.

"I thought you always ate lunch together."

"We used to, but the timetables got changed — the cafeteria was getting too crowded at noon." It was surprising to me how easily lies came to my lips now. Now that I needed to lie.

"Well — you have to eat it anyway, Melanie," Mom insisted. "You know what Dr. Vosch said about gaining weight. And we go to see him tomorrow after school."

I didn't argue any more then. But I didn't eat the lunch either. I didn't even go out to the hillside at noon hour. If I was going to have to eat more breakfast and supper, with Mom standing over me till I did, then what I would do was skip lunch completely. Otherwise I'd just put every bit of puppyfat right back on. After all my work and effort to take it off.

At lunchtime I found a bench in the hallway and sat down on it, and leaned my head back against the wall. I felt less dizzy that way. Though the hall was crowded with kids coming and going, talking and laughing, I scarcely heard them. The cocoon that I'd felt growing around me out on the hillside was there, firmly in place, most of the time now. All the same, as I sat with my eyes half-closed, I was aware of someone coming to stand in front of me.

It was Dan. That was strange, Dan and I never talk to each other in school. But he planted himself in front of me, his hands on his hips, and started right in the way he always does.

"You do know what's wrong with you, don't you, Melanie?" he demanded angrily.

"Wrong? What do you mean?" I answered. "There's nothing wrong with me."

"There is so. I can see how skinny you are now. And I know what's wrong. You have anorexia."

I pulled myself away from the wall and sat up. "What?"

Dan nodded, frowning. "Anorexia. Anorexia nervosa. That's what you have."

I stared back at him, open-mouthed. "You mean — like Karen Carpenter had?"

"Yeah." He snapped the word at me. "And you know what happened to her. She died."

I sat back against the wall again, trying to sort out this new thought. It was hard to think clearly when I was so dizzy. Anorexia? But — that was a disease. I wasn't sick. Or dying. I just wanted to be something special, that was all. And something special meant thin. And I was special — I could discipline myself more than anyone else could. Who else could refuse even a taste of the icing on their own birthday cake?

Dan interrupted these thoughts. "What do you think you're doing anyway?" he went on. "Do you figure you look glamorous or something? Because you don't. You used to be cute — but now you look awful." He hesitated, and then added, "You look really ugly, if you want to know the truth! Who gave you this dumb idea about dieting anyway — "

I stood up. And just walked away from him. I didn't want to hear any more of that kind of talk.

But I ended up hearing more, all the same. Dr. Vosch said a lot of the same things after he'd examined me on Tuesday.

"Blast those newspapers and magazines!" he

fumed. "They write up every darned thing those pop stars do. I suppose you were copying that Carpenter girl?"

"I wasn't copying anybody!" I answered crossly. "I just want to be thin, that's all. You doctors are always talking about how bad it is to be overweight. So why aren't you glad to see someone who isn't?"

I felt Mom touch my shoulder reprovingly at my cross words. Usually when she brought me to the doctor I hardly spoke at all — it was Mom who told him that I had a sore throat or a rash or whatever.

But Dr. Vosch wasn't worried about manners. "You're right — being overweight isn't healthy," he admitted. "But neither is being excessively underweight. Especially at your age. Have you lost your period yet?"

I frowned at him, trying to make sense of the question. "What do you mean?"

"You have started to menstruate, haven't you?" he asked.

"Uh — yes. A few times," I stammered. I didn't like this kind of talk, even with a doctor.

"Well, then — if your period hasn't already stopped, it soon will. By the time a woman loses fifteen percent of her body weight — which you probably have — menstruation just ceases."

I kept my eyes down. If he thought I would be upset over *that* he was dead wrong.

"Anyway," he continued, "your blood pressure is certainly down. And I'll have to take some blood samples for the lab, to check on your electrolyte and potassium levels. They're probably down too — and that can be dangerous. You *must* put some weight back on, young lady."

"I'm doing all I can, Dr. Vosch," Mom put in. "I cook her all her favorite meals — but she just won't eat enough, no matter what I say."

I shifted my gaze out the window, away from them both. Their voices seemed to be coming from somewhere far away, far outside my little private cocoon, and not important to me at all. Even when Dr. Vosch drew some blood from my arm I scarcely felt it. They just don't understand, I told myself. They don't understand that I can't let myself eat those platefuls of food Mom keeps setting down in front of me. If I did that — even just once — I would lose all my control.

Suddenly, though, Dr. Vosch's voice penetrated my thoughts and his next words came through loud and clear.

"You know, Melanie," he was saying, "the

longer this condition goes on, the harder it is to cure. I'm not going to take any 'wait and see' attitude on this. The results of your blood tests will tell me just how serious it is — but I'm telling you right now: I'll give you a week to gain some weight back. If you don't, I'm putting you in the hospital."

"Hospital?" I said. "You mean — the Lakeshore?"

"Yes. There are usually beds available without a long wait in the children's wing. So if you don't change your ways pretty quickly, you won't be a candystriper — you'll be a patient."

"For . . . for how long?"

His eyes bore into mine. "For as long as it takes," he told me.

*   *   *

The ride home in the car was very quiet. I guess Mom was shaken up by the idea of hospital too. As soon as we got home I escaped to my room again.

I seemed to be spending a lot of time in my room. Only somehow . . . it didn't feel like such a safe, secure place any more. I wandered around, automatically straightening the knick-knacks on my bookshelves — Mom's cleaning woman had obviously been in — but even here in my room I felt scared. Scared of lots of things, but mostly of getting fat again. I took the magazine out of my desk drawer and carried it to the mirror. I didn't look as thin as that model yet — I was sure of that, no matter what Dr. Vosch said. So how come it was all right for models to be really thin and not all right for me? If the big beaming smile on her face was any indication, life was just fine for her! She didn't have any doctor scolding her, threatening her with hospitalization if she didn't put on some weight.

The sound of Mom's voice broke into my thoughts. She was talking loudly and angrily — and that was definitely not normal. Mom didn't approve of that tone of voice from herself any more than from Katie and me. I opened my door and crept to the top of the stairs to listen.

She was on the phone. I heard her say, "Rob, I don't care if you have a meeting in a few minutes. I have to talk to you right now! Dr. Vosch has really upset me."

That was Dad she was talking to — and me she was talking about. Were they actually arguing about me for a change? Mom's voice went on.

"Well, of course I'm trying to make her eat.

But you don't know how stubborn she can be . . . Yes, stubborn — your good little Melanie!"

It was strange, I thought to myself, I'd always tried so hard to be good — why did it give me such a thrill to know I was being bad?

"Well, I'm tired of eating problems too!" Mom continued shrilly. "After all, I'm the one who's had to watch over Katie's eating all these years. And now to have problems with Melanie as well — it's too much! I can't do it alone . . . Well, at least talk to her then. You're the one who started it all, you and your puppyfat!"

I quickly stepped back from the top of the stairs. When Mom's call of "Melanie!" came up, I made my footsteps start from my doorway.

"Yes?" I answered.

"Dad wants to talk to you on the phone."

That wasn't exactly true, I knew. He didn't want to talk to me. And for once I didn't want to talk to him. But I came downstairs and took the receiver from her.

"Hi, Dad," I said.

"Now look, Melanie," he said, jumping right in without even a "hello" just as if he were Dan, "your mother tells me that you've been carrying this dieting business too far. That's plain silly, you know."

98

"Well, you're the one who told me I looked so much better without my puppyfat!"

"Oh Melanie . . . " His voice took on an annoyed tone. "I'm sorry I ever brought that word into the conversation."

"Didn't you mean it when you said I looked great? You said I looked great and you whistled at me!"

"Well yes — of course I meant it . . . then. But your mother says you're really much too thin now. Too thin isn't pretty, you know."

"I don't think I'm too thin."

"But Dr. Vosch says you are, your mother told me so. Look Melanie, I have to go now — I'm late for a meeting. I'll call you back later. And — eat some dinner for your mother, okay?"

I hung up without saying yes or no. Mom's eyes were fixed on me and her lips were tight. But then, quickly, she put on a bright smile.

"I'm cooking chicken for supper, Melanie," she said. "What would you like with it — french fries? Or noodles? I'll make anything you want. How about that Parmesan rice you raved about?"

I didn't return the bright smile. "I don't know," I muttered.

"Well, just choose. I'll make whatever you want."

"I don't know! I don't want any of them!"

"Oh. Well — you used to like them all. But if you want something different . . . What would you like then?"

"I don't *know*!"

I was yelling again. Yet Mom didn't reprove me at all. She just said, "Okay, then, I'll surprise you. You go and lie down till suppertime."

And at supper, while Mom talked smilingly about how good everything tasted (she'd made a fancy noodle dish to go with the chicken) Katie was strangely quiet. I guess perhaps Mom had told her what Dr. Vosch had said. Anyway, she hardly said a word.

It was nice to have Katie less battlesome at mealtimes. And nice, too, to have Mom meet me at the door when I came in from school the next day, offering me an after-school snack and sitting down with me while I ate, just the way she used to when I was in kindergarten. I felt . . . important. But I just couldn't eat all that Mom put down in front of me. I couldn't even eat half of it. It hurt my stomach. And besides . . . there was this little voice inside me that said if you start eating everything again, then pretty soon all this attention will stop, you know.

And anyway, I didn't want to gain my weight

back! I wanted to look just like my magazine model — and I didn't yet. I wasn't even as thin as the actresses I saw on television. They all looked thinner than I was — so how come no one was bugging them to gain weight? It wasn't fair.

*   *   *

The next evening right after supper there was a knock at the door. When I opened it, there was Dan again.

"I'd like to talk to you, Melanie," he said.

He sounded very formal, not like Dan at all. And not angry either, the way he'd been when he confronted me at school. I led him into the living room and we sat down.

"I've been reading about anorexia, Melanie," he began calmly. "I got a book out of the library. And I've learned a lot, so I know there's no use just getting annoyed with you and telling you to stop being so stupid. I know that by now you've reached the stage of 'starvation mentality' — so you really can't think clearly any more."

"What are you talking about?" I said hotly. I was the one getting angry this time, with the nonsense he was spouting. "Are you saying that I'm loony?"

"No, not loony," he answered, still calm. "But

101

the book I was reading explained a lot: it said that if you're really undernourished for a long time, then that affects your brain function. You start to have a one-track mind, you can't help it. So it's not just stubbornness with you now — your body won't let you think sensibly."

"I'm thinking just fine!"

"No, you're not. You're sick. And you may have to be put in the hospital."

At that I jumped up from my chair. "You've been talking to Mom!" I accused him. "She put you up to this!"

"I have not. It's all in the book I was reading. And in the hospital they'll probably use behavior modification on you."

"They'll use what?" I drew back from him a moment. "What's that? You mean . . . brain-washing or something?"

"Of course not. Behavior modification means that when you're first put in hospital you aren't allowed to have phone calls or television or a radio or anything at all. I guess they let you read maybe, but nothing else. You just lie in bed alone in your room and eat your meals. Then, as you start to gain weight, you get some privileges back with each bit of weight you gain — one visitor a day, or one hour of TV or one phone call."

I sat down again and stared at the floor and thought about what Dan was saying. Was that why Dr. Vosch wanted to put me in the hospital? If it was, then his scheme wouldn't change me. Lying alone in a hospital room didn't sound that bad. If that was all they'd do to me in the hospital, maybe I could still stay thin. If Dr. Vosch really meant what he'd said.

He had meant it. He wasn't bluffing. Mom took me back to see him the next Tuesday. He hardly spoke a word as he weighed me and checked my blood pressure and drew more blood samples.

But less than a week later I was one of the patients in the children's wing of the Lakeshore Hospital, lying in bed in one of those clown-papered rooms.

8

Dr. Leeman

The pattern of smiling clown faces on the wall-paper of my room didn't have any cheering effect on me, not one bit. Instead, they seemed to be mocking me with their silly vacant grins. Now that I was actually here I was scared.

What would they do to me in the hospital? Would they stick intravenous tubes in me and force nourishment into me that way? As a can-dystriper I'd seen lots of people lying in bed with intravenous tubes in them — IV, we called it non-chalantly. But those people on intravenous were sick. They looked sick. I wasn't sick, I just wanted to be thin! As thin as all the actresses and models on television, the ones everyone admires so much. I just wanted to be admired too. Something had gone very wrong, and I was still trying to figure out what — because when I first started to lose weight I had gotten the admiration and notice that I wanted. But now . . . now they were going to steal my thinness away from me. The one thing that made me feel special — and they were going to take it away.

I didn't even know who "they" were. "A therapist," Dr. Vosch had told Mom — whatever that was. Well, that therapist could just go jump in the lake! I wasn't going to get fat, not for anybody, not for any reason. Uh-unh. No way.

I could feel myself getting angry all over again. I didn't want to start crying though, so I left the bed and began arranging my things on the dresser and bedside table. Not that anything needed tidying. I hadn't brought much. Mom had packed for me: a new pink bathrobe with slippers to match (she wanted me to look well-dressed, at least), some nighties and the pair of warm pyjamas I had on, hairbrush and handmirror and toothbrush, deodorant and scented soap, a few magazines and paperbacks, and one stuffed animal — for company, I guess. There wasn't much to arrange.

I picked up my handmirror and looked at myself. The face that stared back at me didn't seem to be mine at all. In these strange surroundings my face seemed strange and unreal too. Who am I, anyway? I wondered. I'm Melanie Burton — but who is that really? In my own surroundings I knew who I was: a good quiet girl, with shoulder-length brown hair, who was never in trouble at school, who always tried for a perfect report card so that Mom and Dad would be pleased. As I thought about that, it seemed to me that the times when I got a good report card were the only times I really felt like me. Probably because those were the times Mom and Dad paid the most attention to me. The rest of the time, when the focus was on Katie, Katie, Katie, I didn't feel like much of anything.

And now? Now that Mom was hovering over me, coaxing and arguing — even crying over me as she hung my clothes in the hospital closet — was I more of a me? I didn't know. I just didn't know.

A knock at the door made me put down my handmirror. I looked over warily, wondering if this would be "they". But then my eyes opened wide in surprise. For in the doorway was my mystery woman, the one with the long dark hair who'd come to my rescue with Mr. Tanner — a lifetime ago, it seemed.

She smiled at me and said hello. But then her eyes widened too. "Well — hello," she said again. "I remember you. You're the quick-thinking candystriper."

I nodded in reply, and she came in and perched herself casually on the arm of the one big chair in the room. She was so short that one foot dangled, and only her white lab coat made her look old enough to be part of the hospital staff.

"I didn't realize that 'Melanie Burton' was someone I already knew," she went on pleasantly.

Though she didn't seem like "they", I was still feeling wary. I stared back, without smiling, and said, "Yes, I'm Melanie. But who are you?"

"Oh!" She gave a little laugh. "I'm sorry — I forgot to introduce myself. I'm Dr. Leeman, and I'm going to be looking after you here. My friends call me Lee — you can too, if you like. I hope we'll be friends."

I digested that speech in silence. Call a doctor "Lee"? I couldn't see myself doing that. Instead, I frowned and said, "You said you're going to be looking after me. How? By locking me in this room like a prisoner that has to be punished? I've been told that's what will happen."

Dr. Leeman shook her head.

"You're not locked in," she answered, still pleasantly. "You can walk around the ward if you feel strong enough, and you can phone home every evening. But it's better if you don't have any visitors for a while." She stopped swinging her foot and leaned forward. "We're not punishing you, Melanie, by putting you in hospital like this. That's not the reason for it at all. All we're doing, for a while, is getting you out of the environment where you developed your problems."

I jerked myself upright. "I don't have any problems!" I snapped. "It's everybody else who thinks there's a problem. I just want to be thin!"

Dr. Leeman nodded. "Yes," she agreed, "I know you want to be thin. I know that. And I know you're afraid, really afraid, of being fat. But you see, Melanie, right now you've lost so much body weight that your brain is actually malnourished. You just cannot think as clearly as you normally do."

I started to frown again. That was what Dan had told me, and I simply hadn't believed him.

But she was going on. "You really cannot see that 'thin' is okay — but 'too thin' is dangerous. So for now you must trust me to decide what's right for you, to help you gain back a little weight — just enough so that you can think clearly again. Have you found yourself not being able to concentrate lately — on reading, or homework?"

I dropped my gaze to stare at the sheets. I

had, I certainly had, but I wasn't going to admit it to her.

Dr. Leeman seemed to take that for an answer — and maybe it was at that. "I'm sure you'd like to feel less uncomfortable, you'd like to lose that gnawing pain in your stomach — if you could believe it was safe to do so. Wouldn't you, Melanie?"

I didn't answer that either. Instead I asked, "What if . . . what if I don't gain some weight back? What then?"

Dr. Leeman looked solemn. "Then we would have to keep you right in bed, and not allow any walking around, or phone calls, or television."

"So I would be a prisoner, then!"

"No. Not a prisoner. Just a girl with too many problems, problems that she doesn't know how to solve."

"But . . . I can't eat. I really can't!"

"I know," she said quietly. "I know. But I'll help you. We have to retrain your stomach, so that it will accept normal amounts of food again. I'll help you to eat the right amounts, little by little." She leaned forward and looked straight into my eyes. "I won't let you get fat, Melanie. You can trust me on that."

Her eyes were dark and very earnest. Too

earnest — I dropped mine to the sheets again. It was hard to think under that steady gaze, hard to know what to make of her.

She waited a moment and then went on. "But for now, Melanie, you do have to gain some weight, right away. Not too much, I promise. Not enough to make you fat. But enough so that we can start to talk about your real problems."

I looked up again. "My real problems?" I repeated.

"Yes." She nodded, several times. "This excessive weight loss is only a side effect, a smoke screen. It's not the important thing."

That didn't make sense to me at all. And my head was starting to feel dizzy and queer again. I plunked myself back down on my pillow. "My real problem is that nobody will let me be thin!" I shouted.

I could feel the tears welling up the way they always did when people talked to me about my weight. But Dr. Leeman didn't tell me to stop crying. She put one hand on my shoulder while I cried for a bit, and then took some tissues from the box and wiped my eyes, very gently.

"Trust me, Melanie," she said softly, and then left.

*   *   *

I lay back on my pillow clutching the wad of tissues, the tears still trickling. There seemed to be so much to cry about nowadays. The way I felt, for one thing — because I was physically uncomfortable most of the time, just as Dr. Leeman had guessed. And cold. I pulled the covers higher around my shoulders. And just . . . miserable. This wasn't at all the way my daydreams had gone. In my fantasies, when I was thin enough I was going to be admired, and popular, and happy. Not lying in a hospital bed, sniffling.

Outside in the hall I heard a sudden swell of noise, of nurses' cheerful voices talking back and forth. It must be three-thirty, I thought: time for the evening shift of nurses to come on duty and the day shift to leave. The two shifts would go over all the patients' charts together and discuss any change in their condition — I'd seen them doing that lots of times as a candystriper. And then, I knew, a nurse from the evening shift would go around to the rooms and check on each patient. Sure enough, a few minutes later my door was pushed open again.

It was a nurse I'd seen a few times before. I'd noticed her especially because of her carrot-red hair, and her nice cheery laugh too. She recognized me as well.

"Well, hello," she said brightly. "Haven't I seen you somewhere before?"

"Yes," I told her, "I'm . . . I was a candystriper." I didn't actually know whether I still was one, or whether I'd been taken off the list.

"That's it! I knew I'd seen you before."

The nurse walked over to my bed and glanced down at my name bracelet — the sturdy plastic bracelet that's put on every patient as soon they're admitted. And right away I could see her expression change. "Oh," she said, not nearly as brightly, "You're Melanie Burton."

I could guess what had happened. She'd studied the charts at the nurses' station when she came on duty, including one for Melanie Burton. And now she was remembering what else was on the chart: "Diagnosis — anorexia." That tight-lipped expression which had come over her face — I'd seen it before, on Mom and Dr. Vosch. I'd even heard it, in Dad's voice last night, when he'd spoken to me again on a crackling overseas line, saying, "Melanie, you have to stop being so silly."

I turned my head away and closed my eyes. I had to squeeze them hard to keep the tears from starting up again, and after a moment I heard the nurse walking away. I lay there, eyes still closed, and I guess I dozed for a while — because the next thing I heard was the cart with the supper trays being trundled down the hallway, and the clatter of trays being shifted about. And soon afterwards the red-haired nurse came in again, with a tray in her hands.

That was unusual. The meal trays were usually taken around by the ward aides, not by the nurses. I stared at her, and at the tray. What would be on it?

The nurse put my tray down on the over-the-bed table and swung it in front of me. "Here's your supper," she said brusquely. "I have to stay in the room and watch you eat."

That jolted me off my pillow. I sat up with a jerk. "Watch me?" I said.

"Yes," she answered. "Doctor's orders. To make sure you do eat."

The answers came out clipped and brief. She lifted the covers from my tray and then sat down in the chair by the window — rather noisily, as if to emphasize that she had better things to do with her time — while I stared down at my tray. It looked like a normal-sized meal, neither more nor less than was usual. The main dish was chicken pie. I used to really enjoy that in the cafeteria, I remembered. I used to enjoy all the food there. But now, a whole meal facing me all at once — soup, dinner, dessert, drink, bread and butter — and with a nurse watching me. How could anyone eat this way?

Tears prickled at my eyes again. "Doctor's orders," the nurse had said. Which doctor — Dr. Vosch? Or . . . Dr. Leeman? I had really liked my mystery woman in the white lab coat that day so long ago. Or at least I had thought I would, if I ever saw her again. But she was like everyone else. She wanted me fat too. She couldn't stand me being thinner than she was, and more disciplined. And more pure.

The silence in the room was thick as I stared at my supper tray. I could feel the nurse's angry eyes on me. In the silence Dr. Leeman's words came back to me: "We'll talk about your real problems," she'd said.

What did she mean by that? What *were* my real problems, anyway?

9

Someone to trust?

I didn't have a nurse watching me eat the next morning. The nurses had too much to do on the morning shift, I guess. But it was a nurse, not a ward aide, who brought in my breakfast tray — and I got another lecture from her.

"You must eat, you know," she told me. She was a pretty, dark nurse, and not one I knew from candystriping. "If you lose any more weight you'll have to be kept right in bed. And you absolutely have to drink all the liquids on your tray — you must take in eight glasses of liquid a day. Otherwise you'll be put on intravenous, to prevent dehydration."

She didn't sound as angry with me as the nurse from the evening before, but she certainly didn't act very friendly either. She just set down my tray, took off the cover, and with a parting, "Remember — all the liquids," left briskly.

I stared down at this new tray. So being put

on intravenous was a threat, as I'd feared. Well, I didn't want that, so I lifted the juice and milk from my tray onto my swing-table. Then I had to decide about the rest, as I always did now: what things I would let myself eat, and how much of each item. After some deliberation I lifted the dish of cream of wheat onto the table and divided it exactly in half — I'd eat half of that, I decided. There was a fried egg and some cold toast that looked awful, but the muffin looked okay so I divided it exactly in four, and then put the plate with two muffin quarters on the swing-table too. The rest of the tray I carried across the room to the dresser.

As I spread out my napkin on the swing-table and arranged the things I was going to eat into a neat symmetrical pattern, I tried to figure out how many calories I would be getting in this breakfast. Strangely, I couldn't quite remember those calorie charts. Yet I'd known them by heart not long ago. As I ate, I could hear some chirpy children's voices out in the hall. I always liked coming to this ward as a candystriper — and the nurses had liked me then. But now — the only smile I'd had since I got here was from the blue-clad ward aide who'd come in to mop the floor. And the one from Dr. Leeman. She'd sounded friendly — but I bet she doesn't like me either, I thought.

I felt so alone in this strange room, without all of my familiar possessions around me. And why couldn't I remember how many calories were in a bran muffin? Dr. Leeman had said something about my not being able to think clearly now, because I'd lost too much weight. But that was ridiculous. All those models and actresses on television and in magazines — what about them? They looked bright and clear-headed enough. It was very confusing. Too confusing to try to sort out. It was easier to just lie in bed and doze and not think at all.

When I'd finished my breakfast I did doze on and off most of the morning. Again it was the noise of the meal trolley that roused me. This time when my door opened it was Dr. Leeman who came in. With two trays, one on top of the other.

I reared up in my bed. "I can't eat two trays!" I shrieked.

"No, no," said Dr. Leeman, smiling. "One is for me. I'm going to have my lunch with you today."

"You mean you've come to watch me eat! To spy — like that old carrot-top nurse last night!"

Dr. Leeman paused as she maneuvered the trays about. "Did you have a nurse watching you eat last night?"

"Well, sure — she said it was doctor's orders."

"Not my orders, Melanie," she answered. "And I'm not here to watch you now. Just to keep you company. Eating is more fun with some company."

I said nothing to that. Could I believe her? She put one tray on my swing-table and took off the cover.

"Let's see what we've got today. Soup," she began, bending over to sniff at it, "cream of chicken, I think. And an egg salad sandwich, coleslaw, fruit cup, milk . . . oh, and crackers for the soup." She pointed to them as she named them — but then went on. "And how much of this do you feel you want to eat?"

I glanced up, startled. No one had asked me that about a meal before. Could she read my mind?

"How much?" I repeated, a bit stupidly.

She nodded. "Yes — I know it's difficult for you to eat a lot right now. You probably feel very bloated and uncomfortable after a meal, and we have to go slowly at getting your stomach used to normal amounts of food again. So — how much of this would you be comfortable with? Would half the sandwich be about right?"

I looked at the sandwich. It wasn't too thick. "I . . . guess so," I muttered.

"And the soup — could you eat the soup? You do have to get fluids into you — "

"I know!" I broke in angrily. "Or you'll stick tubes in me!"

"I hope not, Melanie," said Dr. Leeman. "I really hope not."

She sounded as if she meant it. And she was calling me "Melanie" a lot, I noticed. Did she expect me to call her "Lee" in return? Because I wasn't going to. I just didn't call her anything.

Dr. Leeman was going on. "Okay for the soup, then," she said pleasantly, taking it from the tray and setting it on my swing-table, along with the sandwich plate with half the sandwich on it. "And the milk too — okay?"

"I guess so." I was agreeing to everything, it seemed. Was she just trying some new kind of trick? "Not the coleslaw, though," I put in.

"Okay," she agreed cheerfully, "not the coleslaw. It takes too much chewing. But the fruit cup would slide down easily — okay for the fruit cup?"

I nodded, and she added that to my table, and carried the rest of my tray over to the dresser — just as I'd done at breakfast. But what she did next really surprised me. Because, as I watched, she cut my half sandwich into four and arranged those pieces symmetrically on the plate, and placed that plate and the other dishes in an exact row, and lined up the napkin squarely against the edge of the table — exactly the sort of things I always had to do myself before I started eating!

I looked on, amazed. How does she know I always have to do that? I wondered. But I didn't say anything. And when she'd arranged everything to her satisfaction she turned to face me.

"It's quite safe to eat that much, Melanie," she told me. "I know, that in spite of what people are saying to you, you still feel too fat. But right now, until you're able to think clearly again, you have to let me do your deciding for you. I won't let you get fat — so it's safe to eat what's there in front of you. Trust me on that."

Then she went over to the big chair, with her own tray on her lap, and started to eat her lunch. She kept up a cheery conversation as she ate but she didn't talk any more about food at all — just about candystriping and the hospital and some funny experiences she'd had.

I didn't contribute much to the conversation. I was too busy wondering how she seemed to know, so often, exactly what I was thinking. About wanting my dishes arranged properly, about not feeling safe if I ate. I would have liked to ask her how she knew — only I didn't want to act like a real pushover for her.

All the same, I couldn't help thinking how nice it would be — to believe her, to let her take over and not have to make any decisions. If only I really could trust her.

*　　*　　*

That evening I put on my new bathrobe and slippers and went down the hall to the nurses' station. As she was leaving, Dr. Leeman had told me I could call home every evening — if I wanted to. I didn't have to, she said, because she would be calling Mom regularly. But I could if I wanted. So I went along the hall to the nursing station telephone and dialed my home number.

I was shivering a bit as I stood there. This fancy new bathrobe wasn't as warm as my old quilted one. In a moment Mom answered.

"Mom? It's Melanie."

"Melanie! Oh, Melanie — How . . . how are you?"

"I'm fine."

"You're fine?"

"Yes. Just fine. It's silly for me to be taking up a hospital bed, that's for sure," I added pointedly.

Mom side-stepped that remark. "Dr. Leeman called us today," she said instead. "She's nice, isn't she?"

"Mmmm . . . I guess so." I gave a shrug, which Mom couldn't see, of course. But I wasn't going to sound all pleased and enthusiastic about what they were doing to me, Mom and Dr. Vosch and everyone else.

There was a click on the line, the sound of someone picking up the extension and Dad's voice said, "Melanie? Is that you?"

"Dad! Are you home already?"

"Yes — I told you when I left that I'd be home on Friday."

"Oh. Yeah." I hadn't realized it was Friday. Here in the hospital it didn't feel like a Friday.

"This new doctor says she doesn't want you to have any visitors," Dad went on. "Otherwise I'd come right over — you know that, don't you? I wouldn't let any old business reports keep me from that."

"Oh . . . sure. I know that," I said, not very truthfully.

"And the school called today, Melanie," Mom said. "They say you'll get your year all right, you don't have to worry about that."

I gave another shrug. I hadn't been worrying about that at all. School and marks and report cards all seemed very far away. But Dad misunderstood my silence.

"And you'll be all right too," he put in quickly. "You don't have to worry about that either. But . . . but listen, Melanie — you don't think this whole business is my fault, do you? The way your mother does?"

"Well, of course it is, Rob," Mom's voice broke in crossly, before I could answer. "If you hadn't brought up that puppyfat nonsense, she would never have gotten the idea in the first place!"

"She certainly might have!" Dad retorted. "You're the one with a drawerful of calorie charts, and the one who's always dieting and fussing if you gain the least bit of weight."

"And you're the first one to start criticizing me if I do put on any weight! You've told me a hundred times what you think of women who let themselves get fat and sloppy."

My shivering was getting worse. And my legs felt tired, standing like this at the phone. And what I was listening to was only making me miserable. So I did something I've never done before. I hung up. I've never hung up on anyone in my life. I didn't slam it. I just put down the receiver and went back to my warm bed.

10
Louanne

That had been Friday night, I realized, because the next day was definitely Saturday — I heard Bitsy's voice out in the hall right after breakfast. I lay very still, hoping hard that she didn't know I was in the hospital as a patient. I sure didn't want her asking what was wrong with me and if there was nothing wrong then why was I a patient, and all that nonsense. Luckily, her voice went away without her coming in. But afterwards, one of the nurses came in with a box — which Bitsy must've brought.

"There was a package left for you at the front desk," the nurse said, handing me a small shoebox carefully tied up with string.

"A package?" I said, surprised. It had *Melanie Burton, Room 208* printed on it in black marker.

The nurse stood by my bed, waiting. She was

gray-haired, but definitely not grandmotherly. "Open it up," she said sternly.

Her brusque words brought a flush to my cheeks. I knew the nurses had to check on any parcel that came to the children's ward, in case it was full of candy or cookies or something like that. But she didn't have to sound like an army sergeant, I thought angrily.

I started to undo the knots in the string around the package. They were tied tightly and weren't easy to undo. The nurse shifted impatiently from foot to foot.

"I could slide the string off for you," she offered, but I shook my head. I always undid knots, even on Christmas presents, and it was my package. But when I finally had them undone and lifted the lid of the shoebox I was too surprised to go on feeling angry. Because there, nestled in a bed of paper toweling, was Dan's precious black steam engine — the one his grandfather had sent him from England — along with a few lengths of train track.

There was a note in the package too:

I thought this might help pass some time for you. If you push the engine along the track the pistons will work, even without power.
Dan

p.s. Hope you're okay. Your mom says you are.

I didn't mean that about you looking ugly.

I read the note over twice. Lending me his very favorite model engine like this was really generous of Dan, I realized — even though a train on a piece of track wasn't something that would pass a lot of time for me. I took his engine out of the shoebox and set it on the dresser, fitting it onto a length of track. The nurse, satisfied that my package didn't contain anything edible, turned her attention to my breakfast tray. I'd finished eating but it hadn't been taken away yet, and she lifted the cover to inspect. I'd left some bacon — it hadn't been crisp and I couldn't possibly have swallowed that — and some cold toast and two quarters of a muffin, so I braced myself for another lecture.

But instead she just gave a sniff and said, "Well, at least you're not on IV like that other one."

I looked up from arranging the engine on its track. "Other one? What do you mean?"

"Oh, there's another anorexic down the hall," she answered. "Didn't you know?"

The word "anorexic" rolled so glibly off her tongue. I scowled to myself. I'm me! I wanted to say. I'm not just a disease or a label! But I didn't say it, of course, and she picked up the tray and left.

When she'd gone, though, the meaning of her words penetrated. In spite of myself my curiosity was aroused. Another person like me? Just down the hall? What was she like? I wondered. Would she be thinner than me? Perhaps so — she was on IV, the nurse had said. I didn't really want to see someone thinner than me, but I was curious, all the same.

After a few more moments of hesitation I went to my door and peered out cautiously. The hall was busy with nurses hurrying by, a ward aide mopping, and a volunteer in her pink smock — but there were no candystripers that I could see. Anyway, I was allowed to leave my room. I slipped quickly into my bathrobe and slippers and sauntered out into the hall, as if I was just out for a stroll. I didn't know which direction "down the hall" meant. But since the nurses' station was to the left, I drifted off to the right, pausing at each door to glance in as casually as I could.

The first two rooms had young children in them, the next had the *Oxygen in Use — No Smoking* sign on the door, the next after that had a boy who looked about my age. The gray-haired nurse hadn't actually said that "the other one" was a girl, but I was quite sure it would be, so I strolled on to the last room on that stretch of hallway. The door was propped open, and as I glanced in I spotted an intravenous unit hanging on its stand.

This was probably the room then. But at the doorway I hesitated. Could I just barge in like this? Suppose I was wrong? I took a cautious step forward — and with that the girl lying in the bed looked up, and our eyes met.

"Uh — hello," I murmured, taking another step forward.

"Hi," the girl in the bed answered briefly.

There was no show of friendliness from her. But now that I was in the room I could see her clearly — and in spite of myself my eyes grew wide at the sight. She looked awful. Her arms were like sticks, and her neck was all wrinkled and creased like an old, old woman's. Her face was creased too, and her skin was a queer yellowish color. What was worse, the bared arm with the intravenous in it was covered in dark fuzzy hair.

She couldn't help noticing my reaction. But it didn't seem to offend her. She lay there with a strange crooked grin on her face, as if waiting for me to say something more. Then, suddenly, her grin grew wider and she spoke.

"Hey!" she said. "Don't tell me I've got some company. Are you one too?"

There was still no friendliness in her tone. She sounded more mocking than anything else. I didn't answer. I just stared.

"You are, aren't you?" the girl went on, in that same mocking way. "You're an anorexic too."

That stung me into speech. "I'm not 'an anorexic'. I'm me, Melanie Burton."

The girl in the bed shrugged. "Okay — have it your own way, Melanie Burton. I don't care. Anyway, whether you're an anorexic or not, you're not nearly as thin as I am."

There was a note of smug satisfaction in her voice as she spoke. "I'm Louanne, by the way," she went on. "You been here long?"

"No."

"I didn't think so. I've been here for weeks."

"Weeks?"

"Yeah. Could even be months, by now." Again there was that note of smugness. "I've been on IV for ten days. I'm a real classic case of anorexia nervosa. That means 'nervous loss of appetite' — but I guess you know that already. Anyway, I'm old Lee's worst case, I heard a nurse say so. Do you have her too?"

"Who's old Lee?"

"You know — Dr. Leeman."

"Oh. Yeah."

"I figured you would. But you're not nearly as bad as me. I'm a classic case, locked bathroom and everything."

"Locked bathroom?"

I knew I was sounding dimwitted. All I seemed able to do was repeat what this girl was saying. I tried to gather my senses together as I asked, "Why is your bathroom locked?"

Louanne shot me a disbelieving look. "Geez, for an anorexic you sure don't know much, do you?"

"What do you mean?"

She shot me another look, exaggeratedly patient this time. "What an innocent baby you are! It is locked, little baby, so I can't throw up."

"Throw up? You mean eating makes you feel sick?"

"Huh!" She gave a snort that was half a laugh. "No, little baby, it doesn't make me feel sick. The bathroom is locked so that I can't go in there and do this" — she poked two fingers down her throat — "and make myself throw up what they've forced me to eat. It's the perfect way to keep thin, dummy!"

I stared at her in horror. I could hardly believe what she was saying. "But — but that's awful. That's disgusting!"

My startled words brought another snort from the bed. "You're unreal, you know that? Talk about a Miss Goody-Goody."

"I am not a Miss Goody-Goody!" I snapped back. That taunt, with its echo of Katie, was the last straw. "I am not! I just think it's disgusting, that's all."

And before she could say anything more I turned on my heels and left the room.

This time I made no pretense of strolling along the hall. I just wanted to get away from her and back to my own room. I plopped myself down in the chair by my window and sat there, staring at the clouds drifting past, but seeing nothing.

"I'm not like that," I told myself, over and over again. "I don't look like her and I don't act like her. The reason I'm thin is because I'm more disciplined than other people. I'm stronger and . . . and purer. I am. I am."

* * *

I sat by the window most of the morning, my thoughts whirling unhappily about me. Before, whenever I was unhappy, I could always lose myself in a book. I picked up one of the paperbacks Mom had packed for me and tried to get interested in it, but I couldn't. Concentrating on a printed page seemed too much effort, somehow. So I ended up just watching the clouds.

When I finally heard the cart with the lunch trays out in the hall, I was glad the morning was over. Would Dr. Leeman come in and eat with me again? I sort of hoped she might. But a few minutes later a ward aide brought in my tray instead — I didn't even rate a nurse. Then I remembered it was Saturday, and the nurses are always short-staffed on weekends. And doctors are entitled to weekends off too — so I probably wouldn't even see Dr. Leeman again until Monday.

The main dish on my tray was lasagna. When I lifted up the cover it smelled delicious. It took me back to my candystriping days, to the day when the lasagna in the cafeteria had smelled like this — and I'd made myself stick to a skimpy salad for lunch. I lowered my nose to the plate and sniffed hard, drawing the lovely aroma right inside me. And as I did, Louanne's mocking voice came back to me. I could hear her telling me that anorexia nervosa meant "nervous loss of appetite" — which seemed even more mocking now. If that was what the term anorexia meant, it was just plain stupid! It meant that doctors couldn't even name things properly. I hadn't lost my appetite! I was just strong and controlled, that was all. My appetite was still there. If I once let up on myself, I could probably eat this whole plateful of lasagna in five minutes flat. I put my face down close to it again and sniffed some more.

And then, as I was sniffing like that, the rest of what Louanne had told me crept back into my mind. About eating what she was forced to eat — and then bringing it up again. I even remembered what she'd called it: "the perfect way to stay thin."

11
An angry explosion

Remembering her words, and that ugly action of poking her fingers down her throat, I felt a shudder go through me. My own stomach is the type that hardly ever gets upset enough to throw up. The only time I even remember throwing up was once when I'd had a bad bout of stomach flu. And I'd really hated the sensation of my stomach turning over like that. It had felt as if my stomach was actually, literally, turning right over. It was an awful feeling, the feeling of your own insides being out of control.

But all the same — awful feeling or not — I had to admit that Louanne's solution was rather neat. It would keep "them" happy — the nurses and Dr. Leeman and Mom and Dad and everybody — because I'd be eating everything on my tray. And I could keep myself happy too, because I wouldn't get fat.

I sniffed at the lasagna once more. Should I? Could I? I didn't really know. I picked up the plate and, still undecided, went over to the chair and sat down with it on my lap. And took one forkful.

It slid down easily, and it tasted good too. I took another forkful. I hadn't even bothered to divide the serving into four portions first, I realized. And I wasn't eating according to any pattern. I just ate. My stomach began to feel a bit strange, since this was more solid food than it was used to. It even hurt, sort of. But that wasn't going to last long anyway, I told myself. I finished the whole plateful quickly, and drank up the milk and juice from the tray as well.

Then I began to wonder — how long should I wait before . . . doing anything? Should I do it right away? Or wait a while? I had no idea — and I certainly couldn't ask Louanne.

I stood at my door and listened. The hallway was quiet. Since it was lunch hour, half the nursing shift would be down in the cafeteria — so this would be a good time to . . . do it.

I went into my bathroom and closed the door carefully. It was a bare little room with nothing much in it except for my toothbrush and toothpaste and the scented soap Mom had packed for me. I turned my head away from the mirror; somehow I didn't want to see myself just now. And then I began to wonder: how was I going to do this anyway? Louanne had poked two fingers down her throat. Was that the way? I guess it would have to be; I didn't know any other.

Rather self-consciously, I knelt down by the toilet bowl. Then I took a deep breath and poked my fingers down my throat. At first nothing happened. I poked again, reaching further down my throat — and then I felt the awful tearing sensation of my stomach heaving as I threw up everything I'd eaten. It was just as awful as I'd remembered. I felt shaky, unable to get up from my kneeling position. And I was only too aware of the nasty sour smell that now filled the little room.

Then I became aware of something else. Something much worse. All of a sudden, as I knelt there by the toilet bowl, the bathroom door opened. And there stood Dr. Leeman, staring down at me with a look of infinite sadness in her eyes.

I froze right where I was, on my knees. *No, no, no!* my mind screamed, as I turned my head away and waited for the angry words that would surely lash out at me — angry words that I fully deserved.

But no words came, angry or otherwise. There was only silence in that bare smelly bathroom as I leaned weakly against the wall beside me. Then, after a long pause, Dr. Leeman spoke.

"Is this the first time you've tried it, Melanie?" she asked quietly.

Eyes closed, still leaning against the wall, I nodded.

"Did you, perhaps, meet Louanne?"

In spite of my weakness I glanced up in surprise. How had she guessed that? But I looked away again just as quickly. I couldn't face her sad eyes. I felt so . . . soiled.

Dr. Leeman's quiet voice went on. "That's always a danger when we hospitalize a patient in the early stages, like you: that you'll meet real hardened cases and become worse. But Melanie," — she took a step towards me — "making yourself vomit, especially now when your heart is already weakened by malnutrition, is dangerous. Really dangerous. You could die from doing that."

She paused, and there was silence again in the bathroom. Then she went on. "Trust me, Melanie. By eating what I prescribe you can gain enough to be healthy again without getting fat. I won't let you get fat. Trust me."

She reached out her hand and touched me on the shoulder. That touch seemed to go right through me, as if all my nerve endings were raw

138

and exposed. As if all my emotions were raw and exposed too, all those feelings I usually kept hidden deep down inside me. Now those feelings came tumbling out: shame, disappointment, fear . . . but mostly anger. Anger that *nothing* ever seemed to turn out the way it was supposed to.

I shook off her hand and stood up, pushing past her back into the room. My lunch tray was still there on the bed table, the plastic cover upside-down beside it, the empty lasagna plate where I'd left it. The sight of that plate made my anger grow even stronger. And without even thinking about it, I picked up the tray cover and hurled it against the wall.

It hit the wall and fell to the floor with a resounding crash. That should have startled me back to my senses — I had never thrown anything against a wall in my whole life. Katie's done it lots of times, but not me. Not good quiet Melanie.

Instead, the sound just made me angrier, and I picked up my empty milk glass and threw that too. I didn't care how much noise I was making. It wasn't enough noise for me. "I hate you!" I screamed, not quite sure who I was even screaming at. "I hate everybody! I hate Katie, and I hate Valerie and her stupid locker and all the stupid kids who hang around her, and I hate hospitals and nurses and doctors. Nothing ever goes right for me! Nothing ever has!" I snatched up my plate, streaked with tomato sauce, and hurled that too.

But the lasagna plate didn't hit the wall. It was heavier than the plastic tray cover, and it veered off to the left. Instead of the wall, it hit the mirror and fell to the dresser.

And knocked Dan's precious black steam engine onto the floor.

* * *

That put an end to my outburst. I stood rooted to the spot in horror. Surely this hadn't really happened. Dan's precious steam engine, favorite of all his trains, that he'd so generously sent to me.

"Ohhh," I moaned. "Oh, no."

I covered my face with my hands and sank down on the bed. This was too awful even for tears. "Oh, no," I moaned again, "what have I done? What have I done?"

I heard the bed creak, and felt Dr. Leeman sit down beside me. And then I heard her calm, quiet voice.

"You've done a very good thing, Melanie," she said.

It took a moment for her words to register. When they did I lifted my head with a jerk.

140

"Good?" I cried shrilly. "What do you mean, good? I've broken Dan's engine!"

"A model train engine can be replaced," answered Dr. Leeman.

"Not this one! This one was sent to him specially, from England."

"Then it can be repaired," she said, still calm. "The important fact is that you just did something you hardly ever do. You were angry — and you let other people know that you were angry. Instead of pushing your anger down and hiding it, you let it out honestly. And that's good."

"You mean it's good to throw things?" I shrieked, waving my arm at the littered floor. "Is that what you mean? You must be crazy!"

"Well . . . " Dr. Leeman gave a small rueful shrug, "throwing dishes isn't the best way to express your anger, I must admit. But the anger itself — that's normal and right. Everyone gets angry at times. And it *is* good to show those feelings and let them out, instead of just hiding them and pushing them down."

I stared at her through brimming tears. "That's not what my mother says," I told her. "Mom doesn't like anyone to shout or swear or — anything. She says it's not nice."

"Maybe it isn't nice, but it's very human.

Humans aren't perfect. No one is. But I think you try to be."

"What's wrong with trying to be perfect?" I demanded.

"People just aren't, that's all."

"It can't hurt to try!"

"It can — if, when you fail, you end up thinking you're no good." She regarded me thoughtfully for a moment. "Tell me, Melanie, what do you want? What would you like for yourself?"

I stared again. "What would I like?"

"Yes. Think about it for a minute."

I turned my head away and my glance fell on the thrown dishes, on Dan's broken engine, and on the open bathroom door. It seemed to me I could still smell the sour odor from that little room. I closed my eyes and said, "Right now I just want to die."

"No," answered Dr. Leeman. "No, I don't think you do. But right now you are doing some growing inside — and that's always a painful process. Grow a little more, and ask yourself: 'What do I want?'"

I kept my head turned away and my eyes on the floor. What kind of a dumb question was that anyway? There were lots of things I wanted: I wanted to be liked by the kids at school and be admired and popular; I wanted to feel pretty; I wanted Mom to fuss over me as much as she did over Katie; I wanted Dad to say I was wonderful even when I hadn't just gotten an A on a test. There were lots and lots of things I wanted — but I wasn't about to go telling them to anyone. I couldn't even imagine telling things like that to a very best friend — if I had a best friend.

Dr. Leeman waited quietly for me to speak. But when I didn't and the silence stretched on, her voice remained kind.

"It's very hard to look inside yourself like this," she said. "I realize that. And it's harder still to tell anyone about the feelings that are in there. But you've already told me some of the things you don't like. You hate Katie, you said. She's your sister, isn't she?"

I nodded — and waited for her to give me the usual lecture about how sisters should love each other. But she didn't. Somehow, she never seemed to say what I expected her to. And now she just agreed cheerfully.

"That's quite normal," she said. "Lots of people feel they hate their brothers or sisters. Often it's because they think that their parents aren't fair, that they play favorites."

"Well, my parents do play favorites!" I burst out. "They aren't fair! Katie gets all the attention. And she gets away with everything! Why, she could throw stuff around" — I waved my hand towards the dishes — "and she wouldn't even get punished. Mom would take her by the hand and talk to her and try to calm her down — and then when I came in, all I'd get would be a 'Hi Melanie'. That's all I ever get."

Dr. Leeman nodded sympathetically. I could feel her eyes on me as she waited for me to go on. But I wasn't used to spilling out my feelings like that and I stopped, embarrassed by all I'd said. What would Mom say if she could hear me?

There was another stretch of silence. Then she asked, "And who is Valerie?"

"Valerie?"

"The Valerie you said you hated."

"Oh, just a girl at school," I muttered.

"And her locker? Why do you hate that?"

I frowned down at the floor. That episode was going to sound awfully silly to a grown-up. "Oh, it's nothing. Sort of a long story."

"That's okay," she said. "I'm good at listening to long stories."

"Well . . . " I frowned some more, but there didn't seem to be any way out except to tell her, so I started in. "Well, you see — Valerie's really cute, so she's got lots of friends. And at our school there's this tradition that on your birthday when you get to school you find your locker all decorated with streamers and posters and stuff. Your friends do it for you as a surprise — if you've got friends, that is."

"And you didn't get your locker decorated on your birthday? Your friends didn't do that for you?"

"I haven't got any friends," I answered.

"None at all?"

"Well — just Rhona. But she's not a real friend — I don't even like her that much. And anyway, Rhona thinks decorating lockers is silly."

"And Dan? The one who brought you the steam engine? He must be a friend too."

"Uh . . . yeah. But he's not a boyfriend!" I added crossly, to prevent the usual remarks. "He's just a friend."

"Of course," Dr. Leeman agreed. "And a very thoughtful friend too. He obviously likes doing things for you — so why didn't you tell him, and Rhona too, that you'd like your locker decorated on your birthday?"

"Tell them? You aren't supposed to have to tell anyone. Your friends just do it for you, that's all."

Dr. Leeman wrinkled her brow thoughtfully. "You can't really expect other people to be mind readers, Melanie. I suspect even Valerie dropped a few hints to her friends about what she wanted." She paused, as if to give me time to think about that, before going on. "You see — if you aren't getting what you want from the people around you, sometimes you have to be willing to speak up and ask for it. You have to tell people what you want. Dan sounds like a good friend — he'd probably have been pleased to do something like that, just for you."

I looked over at the little black engine lying on its side on the floor. I could see that one of the tiny wheels was missing and the piston rods were all sticking out at strange angles. *Not any more, he wouldn't*, I thought sadly. He was going to hate me now. I only had one good friend — and I'd lost him.

12
A surprising discovery

Before she left, Dr. Leeman picked up the sadly broken engine from the floor and even found the tiny missing wheel. I laid them both carefully on top of my extra nighties in the dresser drawer, out of sight. But even with them hidden, I still spent the rest of the day wondering miserably what Dan was going to say. And wondering too if a nurse would be in before long to lock my bathroom door, the way Louanne's was locked.

But the day passed and my bathroom stayed open. And when the nursing shift changed at three-thirty and the evening nurse came in to check on me, not a word was said about my horrible efforts at lunch. Had Dr. Leeman not told anyone? I wondered. Did she really trust me not to try . . . that . . . again? *I* knew I wouldn't. It felt too awful, too gross. But how could she know that? Perhaps — perhaps she thought that if she trusted me, then I might trust her.

That evening the whole ward was very quiet. Being Saturday, there were fewer visitors and no one came into my room at all. Even the everpresent loudspeaker came on only rarely. I could hear it now and again, paging the same two doctors — probably two of the junior staff who'd gotten stuck with weekend duty.

With everything so quiet, I had lots of time to think about what Dr. Leeman had said to me. About showing my angry feelings instead of pushing them down the way I usually did. I often felt angry. But I'd always believed that getting angry was being bad. No one ever told me it was okay to feel angry. And certainly no one ever told me it was okay to show my anger and let other people know I was mad. I couldn't imagine Mom agreeing to that idea. And I didn't like it when Katie got angry and started yelling and slamming about, so other people sure weren't going to like me doing it. And I wanted people to like me.

Then there was the other thing she'd said, about asking people for what I wanted. I couldn't imagine myself doing that either. I'd feel stupid. How could I go up to Dad and say, "Dad, I want you to tell me that I'm a wonderful daughter and you're really proud of me." Or say to Mom, "I want you to sit down and listen while I tell you what happened at school today, and I want you to be really interested."

I couldn't do that. Nobody could. And I certainly couldn't go to Dan or Rhona and say, "Hey, will you decorate my locker for me tomorrow morning?" Nobody does that.

Dr. Leeman just didn't understand. Grown-ups never did.

*   *   *

Sunday started out as quietly as Saturday evening. When the ward aide brought in my breakfast tray I figured hers might well be the only face I'd see for the rest of the morning. So I was really surprised when, just as I was uncovering my tray, Dr. Leeman walked in.

"Oh. Uh — hi," I said, freezing with my tray cover in mid-air.

My heart sank a little — had she come to keep watch on what I did at mealtimes now? Maybe she didn't trust me so much after all. "I . . . I didn't know you came to the hospital on Sundays," I went on lamely.

"I don't normally — at least not this early," she admitted. "But I've been here most of the night. One of my patients became very sick. So, since I was here, I thought I'd drop in on you."

149

Dr. Leeman didn't have her usual white lab coat on. She was wearing jeans and a big loose sweater, which made her look younger than ever. Except for her face — it looked old, and very tired. I waited, wondering whether she'd ask any questions about last night's supper. But instead, she turned her attention to my breakfast tray.

"They've put coffee on your tray," she remarked. "Do you like coffee?"

"No. I didn't ask for it."

"Well, I guess the weekend kitchen staff got your menu muddled." She looked at the covered mug again. "Do you mind if I drink it then? I could do with some coffee."

"Take it," I said, pushing the mug towards her. "I don't want it."

"Thanks." She pried off the lid and took a long appreciative swallow. Then she turned back to my tray. "Scrambled eggs this morning, and a blueberry muffin and toast. And hot cereal," — she lifted the lid on the container — "oatmeal. How much of your breakfast can you eat today, Melanie?"

She spoke in her usual calm, matter-of-fact way. But in spite of that I was still wary. And embarrassed too, so I spoke rudely to hide the fact. "No oatmeal. Yuck!"

"Okay. But the milk and juice stay," she said as she lifted them from the tray onto my swing-table. "How about the eggs?"

"Not all of it. There's too much."

"This much then?" She divided the mound of scrambled eggs and scooped half off the plate.

"Yeah — okay," I said, without much enthusiasm. "And the muffin's small so I'll eat that. But no butter or jam!"

"All right."

I waited to see if she would again arrange my meal for me on the swing-table. And she did. Plates and containers placed just so, muffin divided exactly, even the mound of eggs pushed into a neat circle. What was left she arranged for herself on the tray, though not as fussily. "I'll eat what you don't want," she said with a smile, carrying the tray with her over to the big chair.

She took another long swallow of coffee. But then she noticed that I was just staring, and not eating.

"Isn't your breakfast set out quite the way you like?" she asked.

I glanced down at the swing-table. "Uh — it's okay." I straightened the milk container a fraction. "You . . . you know that I always have to arrange everything just so, before I can eat?"

Dr. Leeman nodded. "Sure. It makes eating feel a bit safer, doesn't it? I understand."

That didn't really explain what was puzzling me. *How* did she know that? And how did she know that eating felt scary to me? I sat there, still puzzling, and she lifted her eyebrows questioningly.

"Uh — I haven't eaten a whole muffin like this, not for a long time," I said, as if to explain my hesitation.

"Oh, I see." She nodded. "Yes, that will feel scary then. And there's something else you may find upsetting, Melanie: as you start to eat a little more, you may notice that your stomach seems to stick out after a meal. But don't worry — it does not mean that you're getting fat. It only happens because your whole pelvic area is so very thin right now. So don't be scared by it. I won't let you get fat."

She gave me another smile and then started in on her own tray. She had half-turned in the chair so that she wasn't looking in my direction at all. "What a lovely big bank of clouds," she remarked, gazing out the window. "They're piled up so thickly you could almost lie down and sleep on them. I once saw a Walt Disney movie where some little cherubs did just that. It was *Fantasia* — did you ever see it?"

I didn't answer. I was too busy concentrating, taking very small bites of my breakfast — one bite of scrambled eggs and then one bite of muffin.

Dr. Leeman went on anyway. "And that cloud over there looks just like a mound of whipped cream. I love whipped cream, don't you? Especially on strawberry shortcake!"

This time I stopped eating. "No, not really. I like ordinary cake best. With icing," I added, remembering my almost untasted birthday cake. I could still see it in my mind. "White cake, the bakery kind, with white icing in swirls along the edges and colored icing roses in the corners — "

I broke off there. I must sound weird, I thought — here I was hospitalized because I wouldn't eat, and then I babble on about rich fattening cakes.

But Dr. Leeman was nodding as if she agreed with every word. "Pink icing for the roses?" she asked.

"Pink and yellow."

"And 'Happy Birthday' written across it in pink?"

"No, in green, to match the green leaves on the roses."

"Mmmm," she said, her head cocked to one side as if she could almost see it too.

I picked up another small bite of egg and then put it down again. "You don't think it's sort of . . . peculiar?" I asked. "I mean, for me to think about food so much? Even though I — " I left the sentence unfinished.

"No, it's not peculiar at all," she answered firmly. "You have to think about something all day; your mind won't just stay empty. And keeping your thoughts on food — food you've eaten, or food you'd like to eat, or how to cook the food you're going to eat — well, it's comfortable and easy. A lot more comfortable then worrying about how to be popular, or how to get people to pay more attention to you."

She put down her spoon and looked at me earnestly. "And it's a lot easier to talk about food than those other subjects too. It's hard, very hard, to open up and talk about what's really on your mind." She paused, and her eyes grew gentle. "I could take a guess at a few things that are really on your mind. For instance, a lot of the time you feel scared, without knowing exactly what you're scared of. And arranging all your possessions just so" — she gestured around the room — "makes you feel a bit more secure. Am I right?"

I kept my face still, but my wonder grew. How could she know so much about my feelings? I sure hadn't told her. I just sat there, and she went on.

"Everybody has their own way of making themselves feel safe. For a lot of people religion does it. Or maybe money. For you, right now, being thin is what makes you feel safe. And as a bonus, being thin — as thin as you are now — is bringing you a lot more attention than you've ever had before, and that feels good too."

By now my curiosity was just too strong. I had to ask her. "Dr. Leeman," I began, "uh — how . . . "

I stopped. She sat quite still, waiting for me to go on. As the pause lengthened, she spoke softly.

"Perhaps if you called me 'Lee' you'd find it easier to talk to me," she suggested.

I frowned down at my plate. I couldn't see how that would make any difference. I took a deep breath and tried again. "How do you *know*?" I blurted out. "How do you know just the way I feel about . . . about so many things? About being

scared and about what makes me feel safer and
— "

I stopped again. This time the pause wasn't
as long.

"Because, Melanie," she said very quietly, "I
was anorexic myself once."

"You?" I was staring openly now. "You?"

"Yes, me. When I first went away to university. I've been just where you are now, Melanie.
That's why you really can trust me, you see."

13
Fat again!

I couldn't quite believe what I had heard. My mouth dropped open and I just gawked at her.

And yet — as I thought about it — I found I could believe it. Knowing that, everything made sense. Of course she would know, so often, exactly how I felt.

The whole idea was rather overwhelming. Dr. Leeman must have realized that too, for she didn't say anything as I gawked on and on. I tried to picture her really thin. Was she ever as awful-looking as Louanne? I wondered. Was she hospitalized? And . . . what was her family like?

There were so many questions tumbling about in my mind. But the one that came out first probably sounded silly to her. "Did you have puppyfat?" I asked.

She didn't treat it as a silly question. "I suppose I did," she told me. "But the big problem was my face. I have a very round face, you see," — she turned towards me to show it straight on — "and so I always looked like a chubby little girl. Still do, I guess."

"I don't think so," I put in.

She smiled a bit ruefully. "Well, it doesn't bother me now. Ever since I was a baby my nickname was 'Pudge'. When I got older and into high school I started to hate that name. And when I went away to university I swore I would never be called Pudge again." She gave another half-smile. "I spent so much time sucking in my cheeks to look less pudgy that I got sores on the inside of my mouth. And it's pretty hard to talk to people and make friends when you're that busy sucking in your cheeks — "

She broke off suddenly and lifted her head. "I think I'm being paged," she said as she stood up.

I hadn't heard anything. But I listened then, and the calm voice came over the loudspeaker, repeating itself as it always did, "Dr. Razinsky, Dr. Razinsky. Dr. Leeman, Dr. Leeman."

"I didn't even hear it the first time," I told her. "Don't you ever miss a call?"

"Hardly ever. After a while it gets so you can hear your own name through your bones."

She set down her tray, unfinished, and walked quickly towards the door. All that morning I kept hoping she might come back. But she didn't. Either her sick patient had gotten worse, or she'd gone home for some sleep. Except for a nurse or two, I didn't have any more visitors at all — until early the next morning, when there was a knock at my door.

"Anybody home?" a hearty voice called out.

The hearty voice belonged to a stocky man dressed in brown overalls. "Hello," he announced as he pushed the door open and marched in. "You Melanie?"

"Yes," I answered.

"Then you're the one with a model engine that needs some work?"

"Oh!" I jumped out of bed, forgetting I was only wearing pyjamas. "Oh, yes, I am! Are you . . . can you fix engines?"

"Well," he cocked his head in a confident manner, "I keep all the hospital engines running pretty well. Where is it anyway?"

"In here."

I hurried over to open the dresser drawer for him. He came and looked down at the tiny black model lying on its side on my nightie, the broken wheel beside it.

"Neat little engine," he remarked. "What happened?"

"It — uh — fell off the dresser." That sounded rather lame, I realized. "It got knocked off. Can you fix it? Can you?"

He pursed his lips doubtfully. "Dunno."

"Oh, try! Please try. It — it was just loaned to me, you see. It belongs to a friend."

"Mmmm." The man looked solemn. "Well — I'll sure try. Hate to see a great little engine like this broken."

I caught a note of disapproval in his voice. He probably suspected that I was the one who broke it. But all the same there was another question I had to ask. "How — how did you know about it being broken? Who told you?"

"One of the doctors came to see me," he answered, lifting the little black model gently in his big hands. "Asked me if I could do anything about it. Said it belonged to a special patient of hers."

"Really? That's what she said?"

"That's what she said."

"Oh. Well — thank you."

"Don't thank me till it's fixed," he replied, and went off with Dan's engine cradled in his hands.

Even though he'd gone I was still smarting a bit from his veiled disapproval. But I was puzzled

160

again too. It must have been Dr. Leeman who'd gone to see him. Had she really called me a "special patient"? How could I be special to her? The only way I ever got to be special was through getting high marks or by being very good — and I certainly hadn't been that!

I folded up the nightie the engine had been lying on and put it away in its proper drawer. My other nighties were all there, quite unused; I'd been wearing the same pair of warm pyjamas ever since I'd been in the hospital. Mom wouldn't approve of that, I thought with a sigh. Why did it matter so much to me, whether other people approved of me or not? Why did I get so upset when someone disapproved, even someone I hardly knew? Katie sure didn't. So why did I?

*   *   *

As it happened, even when I saw her again I didn't ask Dr. Leeman any of the questions that were tumbling through my mind. Because by the time she came in later that Monday I was too frantic about myself. I'd gotten fat! Just from eating a bit more lunch — already, I'd gotten fat!

"You said you wouldn't let me get fat!" I screamed at her as soon as she came in the door.

161

"You promised! I should've known better than to trust a doctor!"

"Yes, I did promise," she answered calmly. "What's upsetting you, Melanie?"

"What's upsetting me? Just look!" I pulled up my pyjama top. "Look at my stomach. It's sticking out! I'm fat!"

I threw myself back on my pillow, my fists clenched in helpless anger. It had happened! "They" had made me get fat. "They" were winning.

But even in my despair Dr. Leeman's next words startled me.

"Here," she said, handing me the extra pillow from the end of the bed. "Punch this. Pound it hard."

I focused my eyes on her still calm face. "Huh? Punch it?"

"Yes. Punch hard," she repeated. "You're angry, really angry. You feel I've let you down. It's okay to have feelings like that — and it's okay to let other people know about them. So punch away. Go on, do it. And shout too, if you want."

I stared down at the pillow she'd handed me. Punch a pillow — what good would that do? How silly could you get?

Dr. Leeman seemed to read my mind. "I know," she said sympathetically, "you'll feel a bit foolish doing it. After all, you haven't had much practice in letting your real feelings out, have you? You've been too busy trying to be good and nice and perfect."

"Well, of course I try to be nice!" I protested.

"Because then your mother and father will love you?"

"Well . . . sure."

"Ah, but Melanie," she said gravely, "don't you see — even if you do hide all your feelings of anger or hate or jealousy, they're still there. You still have them. And because you still have them, because you're not 'perfect', you can sometimes start to believe that you're not worth loving."

With part of my mind I realized that her words made sense. I had believed that. Often. And maybe later I'd think about it. But right now all I could think about was my fat, fat stomach. I pushed the pillow away and looked down despairingly at myself. "I'm fat," I wailed, as my tears began to spill out. "I'm fat."

"No, Melanie." Her voice was suddenly firm. "That's not fat. Don't you remember what I told you: that you shouldn't get upset if you noticed your stomach sticking out like this after a meal?

It's just because your whole pelvic area is so terribly thin that you notice it at all. When your lunch is digested, your stomach will look flat again, long before suppertime."

"Suppertime?" I yelled, my tears flowing faster, "I'm not eating any supper! I'm not eating again!"

Dr. Leeman put her hand gently on my shoulder. "It's scary, I know. And it's okay to cry when you're so scared. But your lunch will get digested soon. Come on," — she took my hand in hers — "we'll walk for a while, out in the hallway. That will make your lunch settle. It'll be all right, you'll see."

She stayed with me for quite a while. Sometimes we walked and sometimes we just talked. She did most of the talking. I was too scared to talk. All I could think of was fat, fat, fat!

Even later, when my stomach looked flat again, I was still scared. I couldn't remember her telling me that this might happen. Had she told me? What was happening to my mind?

14
The boy in the TV lounge

I did eat again, of course. But I sure didn't have much for supper that day. And all the time I was eating I kept pulling up my pyjama top to see if my stomach was sticking out again. Good thing I didn't have a nurse watching me at that meal, I guess.

Later on that evening I put on my bathrobe and went down the hall. While I'd been walking with Dr. Leeman in the afternoon I'd noticed a bunch of children watching the television set in the lounge. I hadn't watched any TV for days and days. Not since I'd been in the hospital, however many days that was. And with reading just too hard for me to concentrate on right now, I figured television might pass some time.

The set, high on the wall, was tuned to a Peanuts cartoon special and a group of small children were sitting cross-legged on the floor in front of it. On the sofa behind them sat a boy about my age.

He was the one I'd glimpsed through a doorway, I realized, that awful day when I'd met Louanne.

Seeing him, I hesitated. Even though I was well covered up, with my bathrobe tied snugly around my waist, still — I was in my pyjamas. Pyjamas were hardly what you wore to sit beside a strange boy.

The boy noticed my hesitation.

"There's lots of room," he said, with a nod towards the rest of the sofa.

Room wasn't what I was worrying about. But I sidled past the children — who didn't take their eyes from the screen — and sat down. The boy turned his gaze back to the screen too. It obviously didn't bother him that he was sitting there in pyjamas and bathrobe. Or even that his bathrobe was decidedly shabby, and too small for him as well. I'd have been embarrassed wearing something as ratty looking as that.

I settled myself at the end of the sofa, making sure my own bathrobe was closed, and started to watch too. I'd seen this special before — it was a summertime rerun — but I enjoyed it anyway. Even if I am too old for most cartoons, I always laugh at Snoopy. The boy beside me was laughing too. And perhaps it was because of his shabbiness . . . but somehow I didn't feel as uncomfortable as I usually did with boys I don't know. Or with any boys, for that matter.

When the first commercial came on he turned to me in a friendly way. "Why do they put the TV set up on a shelf like that? Do you know?" he asked.

"I don't know. So the little kids can't break the knobs, I guess."

"Yeah. Probably. Or so they can't switch channels to some steamy soap opera when no one's looking."

I gave a laugh. "Yeah — that too. Sometimes when I was candystriping — "

"Are you a candystriper?" he interrupted. "Here?"

"Uh — yeah, I think so. I mean, I think I still am."

"Those are real cute uniforms you wear."

"Oh . . . thanks."

"Do you want to be a nurse then — being a candystriper and all?"

"Oh — I don't know. I hadn't really thought about it."

"Or maybe a doctor," he went on. "After all, we're not supposed to assume that a girl who's interested in medicine has to be a nurse, are we?

That's being a male chauvinist, so my mom keeps telling me."

"She does? Is she keen on women's rights?"

"Is she ever! Isn't yours?"

"No."

"She doesn't make your brothers do the dishes, and that sort of thing?"

"I don't have any brothers, only a sister. And — anyway, we have a dishwasher."

"Oh, well — that makes a difference."

I wasn't sure whether it was not having brothers or having a dishwasher that made the difference. But the program came back on then and we both turned back to the screen. It was fun laughing at Snoopy with somebody. And when the special was over, he leaned back with a chuckle and said, "I sure like that stupid beagle. What a character. Do you have a dog?"

"No," I told him.

"Neither do I. The people next door to us have a beagle, but it's a pest — it howls all the time. But maybe that's because it's old."

"Well, I guess Snoopy is pretty old too if you count up how long he's been around."

The boy grinned at me. "I guess he is. I never thought of that. But cartoon characters never change or get older, do they? Charlie Brown's still in the same grade as when he started."

"That'd be neat, wouldn't it? You'd know all the work."

"Yeah. I wish I could stay a little kid like him."

There was an undercurrent of sadness in his voice, and I couldn't help wondering why he wanted to be little again too. I mean, he was a boy and everything's easier for boys. But by then it was nine o'clock; the loudspeaker in the hall was making its nightly announcement of, "Visiting hours are over: all visitors must leave now," and one of the nurses came to shoo everyone back to their own room.

When I was back in my room though I wondered about him, and about why he was in the hospital. And I noticed, with a shock of dismay, how greasy my hair was by now and how wrinkled my pyjamas looked. But then I thought, so what? As if he would care how I looked anyway. That would just be a dumb storybook plot: unhappy girl goes to the hospital and meets a boy, and then all is rosy . . .

With another little shock I realized I'd just termed myself "unhappy girl." Was I? And had Dr. Leeman been unhappy when she . . . got like me? Did she have trouble talking to boys? That was another question I wanted to ask her next time — if I could ever remember them all. I never seemed to, when she was actually there.

Dumb storybook plot or not, on my next phone call home I did remember to bring up the subject of more pyjamas. On that call it was Katie who answered.

"Oh — uh, hi," I said awkwardly. Though I'd been phoning home every day, I hadn't spoken to Katie at all since I'd been in the hospital. "It's Melanie," I added.

"Oh, gosh! Hi! How are y— Uh — " She stumbled a bit, and then said again, "Well — hi, Melanie!"

The conversation was getting nowhere. I guess she'd been told not to ask me how I was. So, more to bridge the awkwardness than because I cared, I asked, "What's new with you?"

"Oh, I went to a great party on Saturday. At Anthony's — you know, gorgeous Anthony."

"Yeah?"

I frowned into the receiver. The last time Katie had gone to a party at Anthony's I'd had to hide my good white sweater from her, I remembered. And now I wasn't around to hide my clothes. "Did you wear my big white sweater?" I blurted, "Now that I'm not there to stop you from going into my room?"

"Your sweater? Gosh, no. It's way too hot for sweaters. And — and anyway, I wouldn't do that! Honest! Why — I even made sure Mom's cleaning lady left everything arranged in your room just the way you left it. I stayed right with her and didn't let her move a thing."

"Oh. You did?"

"Sure. And Mom's bought you a whole pile of new paperbacks and magazines to read."

"She did? Well — actually, what I need most is more warm pyjamas to wear."

"Okay, I'll tell her that. She's probably going to bring some stuff to you soon. I'll go call her now."

Katie, in my room, trying to keep it tidy? I just couldn't imagine that!

*   *   *

After that I did comb my hair whenever I left my room. But I was still wearing my wrinkled pyjamas when, the next afternoon as I was going into the TV lounge, I heard a voice call out.

"Hey — that you, Melanie?"

I turned around in the doorway. It was the man in brown overalls, the hospital engineer. He was coming down the hallway towards me with Dan's engine held carefully in his hands.

"Thought it was you," he said as he reached me. "Here you are — here's your little engine."

"Oh . . . oh, gosh," I stammered, "you've fixed it?"

"Good as new," he said proudly.

"Oh — thanks! Good as new . . . thanks so much!"

"That's okay." He brushed my words aside with a wave of his big hand. "I had fun fixing it. Only — don't let it drop again, okay?"

"Oh, no! I won't, I promise."

"Good," he replied, and marched off down the hallway.

I stood there in the doorway examining the little black engine. It did appear good as new. The missing wheel was back in place, and when I moved it the piston rod chugged around smoothly. And as I stood there another voice spoke close by. It was the friendly boy, still in his tattered dressing gown. He'd overheard my conversation with the engineer and had come over from the sofa.

"Hey!" he exclaimed. "A model train engine! How come he gave you that?"

"Well . . . it got knocked off my dresser, and

that man — he's the hospital engineer — fixed it for me."

"Wow! What a neat little engine!" He leaned closer to inspect it, and put out one finger to move the tiny wheels. "Do you have a big layout at home?"

"No. This engine isn't really mine — it belongs to a friend. But he's got a great layout. He sent me the engine and some track to help pass some time for me."

"You've got track too?"

"Yeah. In my room." I paused and then asked hesitantly, "Want to see it?"

"Sure!"

I led the way back to my room and fitted the good-as-new engine onto the length of track. When I pushed it along the track it did work just as it was supposed to, with the miniature piston rods chugging up and down.

"Gosh," I said, "that hospital engineer must be clever with his hands to fix it so well. How could anyone work on something this tiny?"

"Easy — you put it under a magnifying glass," said the boy.

"A magnifying glass? But then you've got only one hand to work with."

"No — you can buy big ones on a stand, so

you just hold what you're working on underneath the glass."

"Oh. Do you fix model trains?"

He shook his head. "I don't have any; I can't afford it. But I've been to some model train shows. They're great. Have you ever been to one?"

"No. Dan asked me to one once, but I couldn't go."

"Oh, you should've gone. The best show is in one of the Exhibition buildings. They have lay-outs right around the whole room, all joined together and all running at once."

"All HO size? It must be a huge room."

"It is. And if you ask real politely they even let you run one of the trains."

The boy told me all about the shows he'd seen and I described Dan's layout in the basement, including the new signal, and then he told me about even fancier signals he'd seen. And before long I realized I'd been talking to him for a whole half-hour, and hadn't once run out of something to say.

*   *   *

But after that day I didn't see him again. So there wasn't any storybook ending, with me in pretty pyjamas easily carrying on witty conversations just like Valerie. I did get a package of clean pyjamas to wear, but even though I went down to the TV lounge every day for the rest of the week and even peeked into the room that had been his, he just wasn't around.

Louanne was, though. That Friday, when I wandered hopefully into the lounge there she was, sitting on the sofa where the boy and I had sat.

That surprised me. I thought she wasn't allowed out of her room. In any case, I had no desire to talk to her again, and I was turning to walk back out when she spoke up.

"Hello, Melanie Burton," she said, in the mocking way I remembered. "Surprised to see me?"

"A bit," I answered stiffly.

"I thought you would be. But I got bored staying in my room, that's all. So I decided to start eating and get back a few privileges."

I didn't understand quite what she meant by that — though I wasn't about to ask. She must've noticed, though, since she went on to explain.

"That's what they call them here — if you keep on losing weight after you're put in the hospital you lose your 'privileges', and you can't leave your room or make any phone calls or any-thing at all. And that just got too boring. Besides," she added in a self-satisfied tone, "I was pretty sick last weekend — did you know? Real sick. They had to call old Lee out in the middle of the night. I sure had her worried for a while."

This Louanne really is ridiculous, I thought to myself crossly. And out loud I remarked, just as crossly, "She's hardly 'old' — she doesn't even look old enough to be a doctor."

Louanne pulled a face in reply. "Oh, sorry!" she said, with exaggerated emphasis. "Do forgive me — I forgot I was talking to Miss Goody-Good-y."

"I'm not Miss Goody-Goody!" I snapped. "I'm not good at all. Why, I even — "

I stopped myself quickly. I certainly wasn't going to tell her about that episode in the bath-room. Instead I plunked down in a chair and tried to focus my attention on the old rerun of *Gilligan's Island* that was on the screen.

But Louanne had more she wanted to say. She leaned towards me and kept right on. "I've gained a tiny bit of weight, of course — I couldn't help doing that once I started to eat. But I'm not worried. I can still outfox them all."

I tried to concentrate on the program and

shut out her words. I don't need any more ideas from her, I told myself. But then the memory of my stomach, sticking out the way it did now after meals, rose up in my mind. And almost in spite of myself I asked, "Yeah? How?"

She grinned. "Promise you won't tell?"

I gave a shrug that could mean anything. She took it to mean yes and went on.

"It's easy. After all, they can hardly chain me to my bed. So . . . what I do is, I wait till they've settled everybody down for the night and turned out the hall lights, and then I get up and exercise in my room. I have to be quiet about it, no noisy jumping. But you can burn off a whole lot of calories with an hour of hard exercise. So I'll win yet! They're not going to make a fatty out of me! I worked hard to look this thin."

By now I'd given up trying to watch the screen and just stared at her. She couldn't really believe that she looked attractive like that, could she? With her wrinkled neck and yellow face and sunken eyes and sticklike hairy arms? I wasn't like that! I wasn't! And I didn't do gross things like she did either. At least . . . I never would again.

But neither did I want to stay around her any more. Without another word I got up and turned to leave. Her mocking "Bye, Miss Goody-Goody" followed me out of the room. And then, out in the hallway, I heard another familiar voice squealing at me.

"Hey, Melanie! Hi!"

It was Bitsy, in her candystriper's uniform.

"Gosh, Melanie — " she looked as surprised as I was, "it's nice to see you! I've missed you in candystriping. How — uh, you look nice. That's a pretty bathrobe. I love velour robes like that — "

I cut her burbling short. "What are you doing here?" I asked. "It's not Saturday yet."

"No — but I didn't have to write any exams, you see, so I'm out of school now. I'm coming to the hospital two days a week all summer. See — I've earned my cap already. And soon I'll have done enough hours to get a stripe on it. Uh — I guess you didn't have to write any exams either."

Exams . . . the word seemed to come from another life. And so did her excitement over earning a silly stripe. Since I didn't say anything Bitsy hurried on.

"Gosh, Melanie, you really are thin now. I wish I could lose some weight, my big sister is always telling me I should. I mean — I know I couldn't lose as much as you have, but — "

I cut her off again. "Excuse me," I said brusquely. "I have to go back to bed now."

I hurried off to my room and closed the door. I was glad to be alone again, away from them all. The bare hospital room wasn't much of a haven but it was all I had, and while I busied myself straightening the pile of magazines I thought: stupid kid! That Bitsy! Why did I ever like her anyway? As if a dumb stripe on her silly cap was any big deal.

I pushed the magazines this way and that. Would she really go on copying me, I wondered, the way she had with her hair style? Would she really decide to go on a diet too? She probably wouldn't stick to it, mind you — but it would be just like Bitsy to be a copycat again.

15

CA team to Second South

By the time my second weekend in the hospital rolled around I had begun to feel as if I'd been there forever. When I woke in the morning it no longer took me a minute to figure out where I was. The small bare room with its clown-face wallpaper was becoming as familiar to me as my own room at home. Not loved, mind you, like my own pretty room — but familiar.

The hospital routine was familiar too; I could tell what time it was just by what was going on out in the hall. There was the chatter and bustle when each nursing shift changed, the clatter of the meal cart at eight o'clock and twelve o'clock and five o'clock, the sound of mops being swished over the floors during the morning, the patter of hurrying feet when visiting hours began, the calm background drone of the loudspeaker all day long, which always grew a little louder when the end of visiting hours was announced, then the sound of footsteps leaving, and of nurses bringing evening medication and settling all the patients down before the hall lights went out for the night.

After the halls were darkened the hospital became a quiet place, with only the soft-soled tread of a nurse now and again. But quiet or not, that second Saturday evening in the hospital I couldn't get to sleep. The bed seemed too high and hard; I longed for my own small white bed at home. And so, tossing and turning, I was still wide awake when the loudspeaker came to life again, some time after lights out.

"CA team to Second South," came the message. "Any available doctor."

In spite of the urgency of the message the voice was calm and measured, just as it had been that day when I'd been pushing Mr. Tanner in his wheelchair — when I'd first met Dr. Leeman and had wondered whether she could even be a doctor. "CA" means "cardiac arrest," I remembered. Would I remember all the other things I'd learned, if I was ever a candystriper again? Would I still know the routine of the flower room, or how the patient files were arranged, or how to get to all the out of the way departments like the lab and the laundry? Would I still know my way around the main floors and all the wings and wards —

Wards! I jerked upright in bed, as the loudspeaker's message suddenly sunk in. "Second South" the voice had said. That was this ward, the children's ward. I did remember that much.

Only . . . it couldn't be. Cardiac arrest was a heart attack. Children didn't have heart attacks. Had I heard it wrong? Quickly I slipped down from the high bed and went over to my half-open door. But no, I hadn't heard wrong. The announcement came again. "CA team to Second South."

That was absurd. Whatever was going on? I took a step or two out into the darkened hallway. There did seem to be more activity than usual at the nurses' station. And as I stood there one nurse came hurrying from the station, heading towards my end of the hallway.

She noticed me, of course. "What are you doing out in the hall?" she demanded. "It's after lights out."

"I know," I began, "but I heard — "

"Come along." She took me firmly by the arm. "Come along back to bed. It's time you were asleep."

Her voice was stern. Unreasonably stern, it seemed to me — after all, I wasn't doing anything wrong. I didn't know any of the night shift nurses and I certainly didn't like this one, even if she was pretty. But I let myself be led back into my room and to my bed.

"Go to sleep now," she said, and then closed the door behind her.

I hated having that door closed at night. It made the room too dark, too scary, without even a faint glow from the hallway. And there was definitely something unusual going on. I slipped out of bed a second time and crept over to the door and pulled it carefully open again. This time I stayed behind the door. But I glimpsed another nurse and someone in a white lab coat go past, and from the sound of their footsteps they seemed to go right to the end of the hallway.

And then it was quiet. The tiled floor was cold under my bare feet. I listened for a while longer — but before long I began to shiver, and I went back to bed to listen from there. Could "CA team" stand for some other emergency besides a heart attack? I wondered to myself. Perhaps it could; perhaps that was the explanation. There just wouldn't be any heart attacks on this ward, would there? I thought back to the various children I'd seen in the television lounge. I didn't know any of their names, not even the friendly boy — who by now had probably gone home. The only name I knew was Louanne's, and I wished I'd never learned hers.

I huddled there in my bed with the covers pulled up around me for what seemed a long time. I hadn't been sleepy earlier in the evening and I was even less sleepy now. There were more footsteps up and down the hall, but from my bed I couldn't see who they belonged to. And there were no more announcements from the loud-speaker.

At last I got up again. This time I put on my bathrobe and slippers and tied my robe tightly. I went over to the door, looked up and down the empty hallway, and took a few steps towards the nurses' station. But then from another doorway a nurse stepped out. It was the same nurse who'd taken me back to bed before. She saw me again and hurried over.

"I told you," she said, "you're supposed to be in bed and asleep."

"But I can't get to sleep!" I let my voice rise in a weepy sort of wail. "I just can't. I heard that announcement on the loudspeaker and I know what 'CA team' means. So who's sick? I've heard footsteps going down that way —"

I turned and gestured towards the end of the darkened hall, past my own open door. And as I looked, the last door on the hallway opened and a figure in a white lab coat came out.

"Hey! That's Louanne's room," I went on. "Is it Louanne who's sick — again? But then why —"

My voice trailed off. Even at that distance I could see there was no urgency now in the steps of the white-coated figure.

As he came closer I saw it was a young intern, wearing jeans under his lab coat. His face was drawn and sad.

I turned back to the nurse. "What is it?" I demanded shrilly. "What's wrong?"

"Sh-h-h!" The nurse took my arm again but more gently this time. "Hush now — you'll wake the other children. Come on back to your room."

She was a lot taller than me, and easily propelled me back through my open door. But once inside my room I dug my feet in stubbornly. A strange icy feeling had begun to grow in me, an iciness that had nothing to do with the chill of the night air.

"I want to know!" I said, pushing back against her arm. "What's wrong?"

The nurse's arm seemed to falter a little. I took advantage of that to twist around and face her. "What is it?" I demanded again. "Tell me what's wrong with Louanne. I mean — she can't have had a heart attack, she's only my age. She can't be dead!"

At that the nurse's pretty face crumpled. Then it hardened and she dropped my arm angrily. "Of course she can be," she answered harshly. "Don't you know that girls can die of this silly dieting nonsense you're doing? Didn't your doctor tell you that?"

"But — but Louanne had started to eat. She'd gained some weight — she told me so."

"Yes — and that's one of the most dangerous times for an anorexic."

"Dangerous? What do you mean? Isn't that what you're trying to make us all do — gain weight?" I didn't care right then that I was actually lumping myself in with Louanne as an anorexic; I just had to know what the nurse was talking about.

"Of course that's what we're trying to do," she answered. "But all the starving that you silly girls put yourselves through takes its toll, especially if it goes on for months and months. It weakens your heart muscles. And then when you do come to your senses and start to gain some weight, that new weight puts a strain on your weakened heart. So if there's any extra stress of any kind, well — the heart just can't take it."

The nurse paused, her lips working strangely. And a voice that I hardly recognized as my own asked, "And . . . and is Louanne . . . dead?"

The nurse nodded.

The strange voice that didn't sound like my own went on. "And — and what kind of extra stress . . . "

The nurse gave a tiny shake of her head. "We don't know. Any sudden exertion might do it. Vomiting, perhaps . . . though her bathroom was kept locked of course — "

She broke off then. Perhaps she could see from my face something of what I was feeling, and her voice was kinder when she spoke again.

"There, now," she said, "let's get you back to bed. You're shivering. Come on — out of your bathrobe and into your bed, and then I'll go get you a warmed blanket."

I could have told her that a warmed blanket wasn't going to stop my shaking. I wasn't shivering from the cold air now. Dead. Louanne was dead. And what was worse — maybe it was my fault. I knew what kind of extra stress had killed her. Down in the TV lounge Louanne had told me how she was exercising hard at night, secretly in her room. She'd probably been doing that tonight, as soon as the hall lights had gone out. She'd said, "Don't tell anyone — promise." I hadn't promised. So if I'd told someone about it — a nurse, Dr. Leeman, anyone . . .

But I hadn't. I'd told myself she was disgusting, and tried to put her right out of my mind. And now she was dead.

16
A new day

That was the longest night of my whole life.

The pretty nurse, less stern now, brought me the warmed blanket and stayed with me a while. She chatted away, obviously trying to take my thoughts off Louanne. But her words seemed to be coming from far away; they had no connection to me at all. At last, when I finally stopped shaking, she left — telling me again to go to sleep.

But I didn't sleep, not for a long time. And then even when I did doze, it was only to be assaulted by dreadful dreams. In those dreams I kept screaming to somebody: "But I didn't know! I didn't know it could be dangerous for her!" And the shadowy somebody kept answering, "You didn't care, either."

That was only too true. I hadn't cared about Louanne. Never mind the fact that she wasn't very likable — she was still another human being. Another human being who was now dead, and who could have still been alive. And in those hours that I lay awake, I thought of Bitsy again. I hadn't shown any caring for her either. I hadn't cared what it would mean for her if she did decide to copy me again.

Suddenly I sat up and switched on my light. Somehow I'd have to try and stop her from doing that. I didn't know quite how. Maybe I'd write her a note. There was a pencil somewhere in my drawer, and I could use the back of a menu slip to write on. But when I'd found them and had written "Dear Bitsy" — I couldn't find any more words to write.

At last morning came. The sky lightened and grew pink. I heard the day shift of nurses start to arrive, with bright busy greetings, and I got up to stand by the window. It didn't seem right that the day should be so sunny and beautiful. I watched the clouds turn pink, then gray, then white, as the sun rose, and thought about dying. About just . . . not being any more.

I was still standing at the window when I heard the door open. I glanced over. It was Dr. Leeman.

Quickly, I shifted my glance back to the clouds. My heart began to hammer uncomfortably. I have to tell her, I thought, trying to overcome my panic. I have to tell her that I knew what Louanne was doing.

Only the words just wouldn't come. I stood where I was, my eyes on the brightening clouds, and heard her cross the room to stand beside me. She didn't speak either. We both stood silently, staring, thinking.

At last Dr. Leeman spoke. "You know . . . about Louanne?"

I nodded, still silent, and dropped my gaze to the floor. And then the words just seemed to burst out of me. "I know she's dead," I sobbed. "I heard all the commotion last night. And I killed her!"

Dr. Leeman turned to me sharply. She put out one hand and lifted my chin. "What on earth do you mean?" she demanded.

Though my chin had been raised I kept my eyes lowered. "Well — not killed, exactly," I said, realizing those words had been silly and dramatic. "But — but I might've prevented it."

"Prevented it?"

I nodded again. "She told me, you see. Yesterday, down in the TV lounge. She told me she'd decided to start eating, because she was bored with her room, but that she was exercising at night so she'd still stay thin. Only I didn't know! I didn't know it was dangerous for her heart. Not till the nurse told me last night." I swallowed hard. "But I should have told somebody what she was doing. And I didn't . . . so it's my fault — "

"Oh, Melanie, Melanie," said Dr. Leeman, taking my hands in hers, "listen to me. There's no way that it's your fault. Even if you had told us, we couldn't very well have stood guard over her every minute of the day and night. She knew that any exertion could be dangerous for her heart right now. I'd explained it to her. I'd told her she had to be careful, now that she was coming round . . . " Dr. Leeman's voice faltered there. She gave a queer sob as she dropped my hands and turned away. "At least — I thought she was coming round. I thought I'd reached her, I really thought I had . . . "

Though her head was turned I could see that her eyes were starting to brim over.

"Oh — don't cry," I said. "It wasn't your fault."

"But it was," she answered, as the tears began to trickle down her cheeks. "I failed her. I just couldn't seem to reach her at all. And — and look at me now. Doctors aren't supposed to cry in front of their patients the way I'm doing — "

Standing there beside me, wiping at her tears, she suddenly looked so vulnerable. "That's okay," I said quickly. "I mean — I don't mind you crying."

"But it makes me a pretty poor excuse for a doctor. I'm supposed to be the strong supportive one, helping you."

"But — " I searched my mind for the right words, "it's okay. You don't have to act like a perfect doctor all the time. I don't mind if you're not perfect."

Dr. Leeman's head had been bent. But now she lifted it and looked straight at me. Her eyes were still red, but wide open.

"Melanie," she said softly, "do you know what you just said?"

I stared at her, puzzled. "You mean — that I don't mind you crying?"

"And what you said next: that it's okay if I'm not a perfect doctor all the time."

"Well," I was still puzzled, "it is okay. In fact — if you really want to know — I think maybe I like you better this way."

"Oh, Melanie," her voice had a sudden glad ring to it, "and I like you not perfect, too! I like you just the way you are — sometimes angry, or jealous, or scared. I'd even like you messy and untidy and noisy. If only you could start to like yourself not perfect."

I stood very still, hearing my words and hers echoing in the quiet room. I had said that. And I did like her better not perfect.

Neither of us spoke for a minute. Outside the window the clouds drifted past on their endless journeys. I thought about Louanne again, as I listened to my own heart beating out its life-giving rhythm.

At last I spoke. "I don't want to die," I whispered.

"I know," Dr. Leeman answered. "And I don't think you're going to. I think you can learn to like yourself, just as you are, and to feel good about yourself."

"Is that all I have to do? Is that all it takes to cure . . . anorexia?" This was the first time I'd spoken the hated word, I realized.

"No. Not all. Curing anorexia is not that easy. But you have taken one big step towards recovery."

"But — but . . . " I stopped, trying to sort through the thoughts crowding my mind. "But it's only when I *am* perfect — when I'm nice, and polite, and quiet, and get all A's — that Mom and Dad pay any attention to me. It's the only time they love me."

"No, it's not the only time they love you —

after all, Katie doesn't do those things, and they still love her. But you are right about needing more attention from them. That's why I said you have to learn how to ask for attention, in some other way than through being sick."

This time I didn't balk at the word "sick" either. I was too busy getting used to these new ideas. After a moment Dr. Leeman spoke again.

"I think you'll find that you're very likable, Melanie — just the way you are."

"Likable? Just for me, myself?"

"Yes. Just for you yourself."

"But . . . " I frowned, as another thought struck me, "once I'm better you'll leave me. You're the only person who's ever said that to me, and you'll leave me."

"I won't leave you, Melanie. I'll be around as long as you need me. And that may be a long time. Getting over anorexia is a lengthy process, and a slow one. And it's a process that will eventually have to involve your whole family."

"My whole family? Dad too? He won't like that, he keeps saying it's not his fault — "

"It's not anybody's fault," she put in firmly. "When we do get the whole family together to talk, it won't be to blame anyone for anything. It will be to help you all learn to think and act a bit differently."

"Dad still won't like it," I said again.

"Perhaps not. But I think he'll come all the same. He does love you. So does your Mom. And Katie too."

The room grew quiet again as I thought about that. Did they? Did they really? I remembered the packages sent to the hospital by Mom, the postcard that had come from Dad on his last trip, and Katie making sure my room stayed as I'd left it.

I'd had almost too many brand-new thoughts for one day. As I pondered some more, my glance fell on the menu card where I'd written "Dear Bitsy" and nothing more. I still didn't know what to write — but I could ask Dr. Leeman to help me, I realized. I could ask.

Just then the door opened and the ward aide came bustling in with my breakfast tray. The clatter as she set it down on my bed-table broke the silence between us, but neither Dr. Leeman nor I moved. I wanted her to stay, I knew. I wanted to talk with her some more.

"Uh . . . do you have to . . . go anywhere right now?" I asked awkwardly.

I was studying the floor again, but I could

feel her eyes on me. "No. Not really," she answered.

There was another pause while I took a deep breath. Asking sure wasn't easy. "Uh . . . would you eat breakfast with me then . . . Lee?"

I looked up in time to see her smile. "Yes, Melanie. I'd like to," she said.

"Only — " I went on, my voice a little firmer, "if you're really hungry, we should ask for an extra tray. I think . . . I think I might eat all my scrambled eggs myself today."

Dorothy Joan Harris has been interested in language and words since she was a child growing up in Kobe, Japan. After graduating from the University of Toronto with a degree in Modern Languages, she went back to Kobe to teach at the Canadian Academy. She returned to Canada to raise her family, and now lives in Etobicoke, Ontario.

Dorothy Joan's novels include *Don't Call Me Sugarbaby!,* about a girl who discovers that she has diabetes, and *Speedy Sam,* for younger readers. She is also the author of several picture books, among them *No Dinosaurs in the Park* and *Four Seasons for Toby.* She is, as always, working on a number of other books.